THE BODY IN THE COTTAGE

I quickly moved around Ambrose and stepped into the cottage. The minute I entered, though, I noticed something unusual: the smell. Not a normal garden smell like mold or compost or rotting leaves . . . the room smelled like mint. A chemically mint odor, like the kind they used in menthol cigarettes.

I glanced around for the source. The pile I'd spied beneath the window turned out to be a rumpled green business suit and matching shoes.

It was Mellette Babineaux. Her feet splayed out at unnatural angles and her unseeing eyes stared straight ahead. My scream tore through the small space.

"Missy!" Ambrose rushed forward. "Call 9-1-1. Quick!"

But I couldn't move. My feet had become rooted to the ground. Several seconds—or were they minutes?—passed.

"Now!" he said.

That woke me. I whipped out my cell and dialed 9-1-1.

A voice answered before the second ring. "This is 9-1-1. What's your emergency?"

"There's been an accident at the old Sweetwater mansion. Not inside, but outside. We're in a shed. Come quick!"

"Are you with the victim right now?"

Victim? I hadn't really thought about her as a victim. All I knew was that Mellette Babineaux—the one who'd toured me around the house not more than an hour ago—now lay puddled in a heap on a dirty cement floor . . .

Books by Sandra Bretting

MURDER AT MORNINGSIDE

SOMETHING FOUL AT SWEETWATER

Published by Kensington Publishing Corporation

Something Foul at Sweetwater

Sandra Bretting

LYRICAL UNDERGROUND
Kensington Publishing Corp.
www.kensingtonbooks.com

LYRICAL UNDERGROUND BOOKS are published by

Kensington Publishing Corp.
119 West 40th Street
New York, NY 10018

All Kensington titles, imprints, and distributed lines are available at special quantity discounts for bulk purchases for sales promotion, premiums, fund-raising, educational, or institutional use.

Special book excerpts or customized printings can also be created to fit specific needs. For details, write or phone the office of the Kensington Sales Manager: Kensington Publishing Corp., 119 West 40th Street, New York, NY 10018. Attn. Sales Department. Phone: 1-800-221-2647.

Lyrical Underground and Lyrical Underground logo Reg. US Pat. & TM Off.

First Electronic Edition: December 2016
eISBN-13: 978-1-60183-715-8
eISBN-10: 1-60183-715-1

First Print Edition: December 2016
ISBN-13: 978-1-60183-716-5
ISBN-10: 1-60183-716-X

Printed in the United States of America

Chapter 1

Heaven only knows I should have brought back a tote sack full of beignets that day, like I'd planned, and *not* a sales flyer for the old Sweetwater mansion down the road.

But how could I resist something so full up on Southern charm first thing in the morning? Especially when I rounded the last curve before Dippin' Donuts and saw a *For Sale* sign waving at me from the property's front lawn, like a friendly neighbor saying *hey*.

I swerved off the road, my tires spitting pea gravel and chalk dust, for a better look. Ever since I moved to Louisiana to open a hat shop, about a year and a half ago now, I'd been mesmerized by the antebellum mansions that seemed to sprout from the soil here every so often, like elegant daylilies planted in the sugarcane fields by mistake.

This particular mansion sat high on a hill. Two regiments of live oaks lined the front walk, their limbs bearded in wispy Spanish moss and their branches arching until the boughs touched. Beyond this leafy keyhole sat the mansion, which was held aloft by at least half a dozen alabaster columns. Bright August sun glanced off a column to the east, as if God wanted to shine a spotlight there, while the rest of the pillars patiently awaited their turns.

Best of all, a Plexiglas box full of flyers rested against the *For Sale* sign. My granddaddy always said it didn't cost nuthin' to look, so I scrambled out of my VW and retrieved a flyer, which was written in fancy cursive type:

Historic mansion for sale. Built in 1850. Jewel in the rough!

Which was all well and good, but not the most important thing. I found *that* two paragraphs later:

Owners willing to finance. $250,000.

Well, that couldn't be right. A house this grand—surely on the National Register of Historic Places and surely as pretty inside as out—should go for double or triple that amount. A builder would kill for the columns alone, not to mention the expensive iron railing that curled along a widow's walk on high.

Between all that and a wide plank veranda that circled the ground floor like a hoop skirt, the flyer must be lying.

Ambrose needed to see this. Given my best friend was already at his design studio and waiting for me to bring him some beignets, though, I'd have to choose my words carefully and not go running off at the mouth. I dialed his cell and patiently waited through a few rings.

"Hi, Missy. What's wrong?"

Unfortunately, that was the greeting you got when you'd called your best friend so early on a Monday morning. "Nothing's wrong. Any chance you're up for a little drive?"

"Why?" A suspicious pause. "You didn't run out of gas again, did you?"

"No, nothing like that. I was driving along, minding my p's and q's, when I saw that old mansion on the road to the doughnut store. You remember the one? Only now it's got a *For Sale* sign in the front yard, and I'm pretty sure it's a sign from heaven."

His sigh said more than any words could. "Missy, everyone knows those old houses eat money. Best thing you can do is walk away."

That was my Ambrose—practical to a T. Whereas I believed more was more and never less, Ambrose was of a different mind. Bless his heart.

In Bo's defense, he couldn't see the forest-green shutters that bookended perfectly spaced windows or the attic dormers that gazed over the manicured lawn with obvious approval or how the whole shebang culminated in an actual widow's walk. Breathtaking, it was. Simply breathtaking.

"That's the thing." I added my own pause for special effect. "The price is right here on the flyer. Could be a typo, but it's a sight less than what they charge for new houses around here."

"Missy." Out came the voice he used when he tried to protect me from myself. "Think about it. Do you know how much it'd cost to cool a place like that all summer?"

"No." I hadn't even considered the more practical matters, like air-conditioning or heaters or keeping the grass green. "Wait a minute. Someone walked out on the front porch. Wonder if they'll let me in?"

"Missy—"

"Gotta run. Meet me back at the rent house," I said.

Ambrose and I shared what the locals called a "rent house" down the road, although one day I hoped we'd share a whole lot more.

I tucked the cell into my skirt pocket and hurried up the lawn. "You-hoo! You there."

The stranger froze. Judging by the crook of her pale neck and a wispy ponytail she'd feathered over one shoulder—which reminded me of the silvered moss—the old gal was about eighty or so.

"Are you the owner?" My voice boomed in the morning quiet, but I didn't want the stranger to hightail it back inside before we could speak. "I see it's for sale. I'm renting a house down the road with my best friend, and I've driven by your property a thousand times."

I was rambling, but by this time, it'd be plum rude of her not to acknowledge me. That was why what happened next startled me so. Instead of giving me a proper greeting and ushering me inside the house, like any good Southerner would, this old gal turned tail and ran back through the door lickety-split, as if I'd waved a Smith & Wesson high in the air and not a real-estate flyer.

Well, I never. Southern hospitality, my foot!

I stalked to the front door and began to knock, since I never did truck with bad manners. It swung open after a moment, but only because it was manned by someone new. This woman looked to be about my age—or as I liked to say, on the north side of thirty—and she wore a green business suit with matching shoes. Her face seemed vaguely familiar.

"I'm sorry about Ruby," she said.

"I should hope so." It wasn't this woman's fault I'd run into the rudest person I'd yet to meet in Louisiana, but the old gal had wounded my pride. "I only want to peek inside."

"Of course you do. Come on in."

The stranger waved me in, which caused a tangle of bracelets on her wrist to jingle like wind chimes. "Sorry again about Ruby."

The sting of the slight faded, though, the minute I walked through the front door. Hardwood floors glimmered beneath my feet like still water on a bayou, and the walls wore rich panels of striated mahogany. A needlepoint tapestry of herons two-stepping somewhere in the Gulf covered an entire wall, the gentle S curve of the birds' necks like a wavy line of sea foam.

"It's so beautiful!" I said.

"The house was built in 1850. That's before the Civil War."

Slowly my eyes adjusted to the dim light. "I know all about these old mansions."

I'd been hired to work for a bride at one of them some six months back. Unfortunately, I ended up smack-dab in the middle of a crime-scene investigation before everything got put to rights again, but I ended up loving the mansion even so.

Now small details began to emerge from the furnishings around me. Bits of silk dangled from the tapestry's hem like marsh grass, the baseboards beneath it wore decades of scuff marks, and even the front door didn't quite meet up with its frame. *No matter.*

"A wedding planner hired me for a ceremony at Morningside Plantation," I said. "'Course, this mansion's a lot smaller, but that's just as well. I never thought people actually sold these old houses."

"Well, you're lucky. This one's owned by a trust and they're in a hurry to get rid of it. Are you interested? I'm the Realtor here. Name's Mellette. Mellette Babineaux."

She thrust out her hand, which set off the bracelets again and also called up the smell of menthol cigarettes.

"Why . . . I know you." I shook her hand, amazed to meet someone from my past right here in Louisiana. "I'm Missy DuBois. You went to Vanderbilt, right?"

"I did indeed. Thank goodness for those academic scholarships."

"But you were in a sorority too. Weren't you were the chapter president of Pi Phi? I was a coupla years behind you."

She seemed pleased to be recognized. "Ain't that the berries! We're sorority sisters. My godmother paid for that, hallelujah."

"Do you ever get back to Nashville?" I asked.

"'Fraid not. Work keeps me too busy. You?"

"The same. I still have T-shirts from the parties, though. Boxes and boxes of them. Can't quite make myself toss 'em in the garbage."

She smiled wistfully. "I only bought a few. What did you say your name is again?"

"Missy. Missy DuBois. I moved to town about a year and a half ago."

Her eyes widened. "Are you the gal who opened a hat shop in town? People told me that store wouldn't last more than six months, but look at you! It's been a sight longer and it seems to be going great guns. Amazing we haven't met before now."

"Well, not to brag, but Crowning Glory turned a year old at Christmas." Which felt wonderful to be able to say. When I found out Southern plantations all along the Great River Road attracted brides like flies to honey, I set myself up making hats, veils, and whatnot for wedding parties. Ambrose owned the shop next to mine, where he made custom gowns for brides and their maids.

"You're gonna make us all proud," she said. "Maybe you could speak to our alumnae group sometime. We meet once a month at the Junior League."

I was about to respond when the older woman who'd been so rude to me earlier emerged from the shadows.

"There you are," Mellette said. "Ruby here is the caretaker. Unfortunately, today's Monday. You know what that means, don't you?"

I racked my brain but came up empty. "Can't say that I do."

"It's bad luck to be visited by a woman first thing on Monday morning," she said. "In some parts of the bayou, that is. Silly super-stition, if you ask me. As if that would make a difference."

Ruby quickly cut her eyes at Mellette. "Ya bes' not be sayin' dat, madam."

Why, I'd know a Cajun accent anywhere. I'd met a gardener at a wedding a few months back who stretched out his vowels like this old gal.

"You must be Cajun," I said. "French Creole, right?"

"Born in des parish."

Before I could speak again, Mellette turned.

"Where are my manners? Ruby, go get our guest some sweet tea. This humidity is going to be the death of us all. Guess we should ex-pect as much come August."

When Ruby didn't hop to it, Mellette's smile hardened. "Today, preferably."

That made the old woman finally back away, but not before she cut her eyes at the real estate agent.

"That one's a pill," Mellette said, once Ruby was gone. "Wouldn't be surprised if she's got a voodoo doll back at her house that looks exactly like me. Bless her heart. Now, let's start in the drawing room and we'll work our way up."

I followed along as Mellette led me from one room to the next. The rooms were small by today's standards and desperate for some fresh paint and spackle, but other than that, I couldn't see any major flaws. And thick crown molding covered the walls, not to mention cut-crystal wall sconces that reflected light onto them like dusty diamonds.

"I have to ask." I couldn't hold my tongue any longer. "Why the low price? It should go for double or triple that amount."

"There's a bit of work to be done." Mellette shrugged. "And there's been some talk about voodoo ceremonies or some such. Not that this particular mansion had slaves, mind you, because it didn't."

Funny she felt the need to answer a question I hadn't even asked. After a bit, we wandered back to the staircase, where Ruby finally stood with my tumbler of sweet tea.

"That voodoo's all nonsense. Right, Ruby?" Mellette asked.

"If'n ya say so." Ruby handed me the sweating tumbler. "Nobody be doin' dat stuff 'round here no more."

"Well, that's good." I accepted the tumbler and took a sip. Just the way I liked it . . . as sweet as honeysuckle. "Although it's hard to imagine why they'd pick somewhere so pretty to do it in the first place."

"Da place don' much matter, missus. It's all in da charms. Wot ya can do wit' da amulets an such."

"Ruby, you know that's a bunch of hooey," Mellette said. "Let's not give Missy here any crazy ideas, okay?"

It's a little too late for that. "So, when's the last time they had one of those voodoo things around here?"

"Years. Decades." Mellette tried to sound nonchalant, but her pinched face gave her away. "The house has been vacant for many years now. That's why the trust is selling it. They know it needs work, but the heirs don't want to keep it, so it's ripe for the picking. Did I mention there's even a studio out back?"

"You don't say." I followed her gaze to the window. "What kind of studio?"

"Look." She pointed to a whitewashed cottage that lay just beyond the glass. Pink swamp roses ambled over a pitched roofline, and purple verbena ran wild through an abandoned vegetable bed meant to hold carrots or cabbage. I fully expected seven dwarfs to emerge from the bottom of the Dutch door with pickaxes slung over their shoulders.

"It's a great place for someone to work on projects," Mellette said. "There are sweet little hidey-holes like that all over this place."

My heavenly days. The cottage would be perfect for a design studio! Even though the roof sagged some and the door was all catawampus, I could block and stitch and steam hats out there to my heart's content.

"Yep, imagine all the privacy you'd have," she added.

"You can say that again! But I need to talk to my best friend first. Maybe bring him out here for a tour. I trust his opinion on everything."

"Fine by me," she said. "But I suggest you get a move on if you want this place. Someone's bound to come along and scoop it up."

No doubt she was right. Places like this only came along but once in a blue moon. Maybe I could convince Ambrose to come over and tour the house with me and then I could bend his ear about all the wonderful ways we'd renovate it.

Although the morning had gotten off to a sour start, something great might come of it yet.

Chapter 2

If the way to a man's heart was through his stomach, then every-thing I needed lay in a greasy bag of beignets I'd placed on the car seat next to me. One taste of that powdered sugar and choux paste and Ambrose would say yes to anything I proposed. Even to buying a derelict mansion so we could renovate it side by side.

My VW pitched and rumbled on the journey home, the sack of beignets bouncing along. Compared to Sweetwater, the little rent house we shared up ahead looked tiny.

Tiny, but quaint. It had bubblegum-pink walls and a used-brick fireplace, and it reminded me of something Barbie would own if she and Ken ever settled in the deep South. Best of all, I'd planted bee balm next to the front gate when we first moved in, and now hummingbirds and butterflies flitted around the place in abundance. I passed several as I made my way through the gate and into the house.

I slowed as I approached the kitchen. Here, sunshine warmed the buttercream-yellow walls and splashed across a farmhouse table that went back two generations. That was where I found Ambrose, hunched over a plate of scrambled eggs and Jimmy Dean sausage.

"Look at you," I said. "And here I thought you'd starve to death."

His knife clattered onto the plate. "Hey, there. Where've you been? I thought we'd meet up an hour ago."

Today he wore my favorite polo: the lapis one that brought out his eyes. As we said down South, "I can't-never-could" resist a man with long eyelashes, and his reminded me of Bambi's.

"Here's the thing." Our farmhouse table had benches instead of chairs, so I plopped down next to him and laid the beignets between us. "I got to tour the Sweetwater mansion with a real estate agent. Boy, did I learn a thing or two."

"That so?" To be honest, his beautiful eyes kept leaving my face to scope out the oily sack on the table.

"It goes all the way back before the Civil War. Turns out a trust owns it, and they're looking to sell cheap. Do you know they only want two hundred and fifty thousand dollars for it? Never in my life did I think a house like that could be so inexpensive."

"Does it have a roof?"

I shot him a look. "Of course it has a roof. You've seen it. And real hardwood floors on the inside. Looked like mahogany to me. Point is, someone could fix up that place like nobody's business if they had half a mind to do it."

"So it's falling down, right? Maybe that's why they don't want very much for it. Sounds like a lot of maintenance to me."

If there was one thing my Ambrose was allergic to, it was mainte-nance. Didn't much matter if it involved our shops back in town, this old rent house or his brand-new Audi Quattro. He had a hard time looking beyond the elbow grease. Whereas I was the exact opposite. Give me a paintbrush, a rotary sander, and a crescent wrench, and I was happier than a dead pig in the sunshine.

"But you've always told me it's good to have a hobby," I said. "This is something we can do together, now that our businesses have taken off."

What a relief to be able to say that. Ambrose and I had both arrived in Bleu Bayou with nothing more than our designer look–books and our desire to bring high fashion down to the South. Course, Ambrose also needed a fresh start, since his college sweetheart, a pretty cata-logue model, had passed away from breast cancer a few years before.

Now we owned side-by-side design studios, where a stream of brides kept us up to our elbows in netting, silk flowers and, thank-fully, sales receipts.

"Yeah," he said, "but I was thinking maybe we could try line dancing or fly-fishing. Or go off-roading in the bayous. Not renovate an old mansion. I thought those stayed in families, anyway. Why'd this one come up on the market?"

"Beats me. But it's owned by a trust and they want to sell it right quick. That's what the Realtor told me. We could do it together. C'mon, Bo."

He didn't look convinced, so I reached into the sack and pulled out a doughnut. "Beignet?"

He finally smiled. "Now, don't think I'm gonna agree with you because you brought home-fried fritters." He accepted the powdery offering. "I have half a mind to tell you no."

Hallelujah. That meant the other half was as good as mine. "It couldn't hurt to look around the place. I even know the real estate agent. Turns out she went to Vanderbilt too. We can head on over there, poke around and maybe test the plumbing. Aren't you curious to see what it looks like on the inside?"

"Well, now that you mention it—"

He never could tell me no. I planted a big, wet kiss on his cheek to show my gratitude. "I'll grab the car keys while you finish up here. You're gonna love it. I know you will."

The road to Sweetwater seemed busier now. Contractor pickups, windowless work vans, and Marathon Oil tanker trucks cruised alongside us. Once I spied the old Sweetwater mansion, I pulled over nice and easy, so as not to scatter the pea gravel.

Ambrose's eyes widened when he realized where we were. "This is the place you're talking about? It's enormous! But I have to hand it to you, it is a good-looking house."

"I knew you'd think that. And it's not so big when you get inside. It's the columns make it look that way. C'mon."

I hopped out of the VW. Now that we'd hit August, humidity settled over me like a wet bedsheet, so I twisted my long hair into a bun and poked the stray ends in nice and tight.

My plan had been to march straightaway up the lawn and rap on the door—hang the chances of running into that Ruby again—but something looked different.

An expensive sedan sat near the kitchen now. The car's enormous hood fanned across the space and a gleaming chrome bumper shielded its tires. Oddly enough, I'd seen it somewhere before.

"Wonder who's here?" Ambrose asked. "The owner?"

"I told you, it's owned by a trust, and I don't think the heirs live here. But I've seen that car before." A pair of interlocking R's on the hood jogged my memory. "Why, it's Mr. Solomon's Rolls-Royce. Wonder what he's doing here?"

Herbert Solomon had hired Ambrose and me back in May to design his daughter's wedding outfit. He'd booked Morningside Plantation down the road—now a gorgeous hotel—and even commissioned the

Baton Rouge Symphony Orchestra to play "Here Comes the Bride" on the front lawn.

Unfortunately, his daughter was murdered right before the big event. People still bragged on me for helping the Louisiana State Police solve that crime, although any law-abiding citizen would have done the same.

"C'mon, Bo. Let's go say hello."

The front door blew open the minute we started up the lawn. Herbert Solomon barreled through the entry, looking the same as always: a deep scowl, a bulging briefcase, and an expensive business suit, even on a warm day like today.

I panicked and hopped in front of the *For Sale* sign. The last thing I needed was to enter a bidding war with Herbert Solomon over this property. He'd already bought Morningside Plantation and could afford to buy this place with his pocket change.

He spied me and began to trek down the lawn, the designer briefcase slapping his leg with each step. "Well, well." He pulled up short when he reached me. "This is a surprise, Miss DuBois." He nodded at Ambrose. "Mr. Jackson."

"I could say the same." Although I hadn't seen him since his daughter passed away, I'd often thought about his wife, Ivy. While Herbert Solomon was brash and overbearing, Ivy was sweeter than the tea I'd had earlier. Shame on me for not paying her a visit before this. "How's Ivy doing?"

"She's holding up. Some weeks are better than others."

"Please tell her I'm thinking about her. I'll have to pay her a visit soon."

He grimaced. "It might not be easy. She spends all of her time at the Mall of Louisiana, I'm afraid. But I'll tell her."

"Whatever brings you out here this morning?" I asked.

The briefcase in his hand seemed obvious enough, but I hoped I was wrong.

"Business, same as always."

"You're not thinking of buying this dinky place, are you?" My heart stilled at the very thought.

"Haven't decided. My other property's working out pretty good. It's booked all summer, as a matter of fact. Thought I might be able to work out a deal here."

"But this one's so much smaller than Morningside." I tried to keep my voice level. "And not nearly as grand. Don't those brides expect the world these days?"

He shot me a funny look. "I guess so. What are *you* doing here?"

"Nothing. Curious, more than anything else."

"You're wasting your time," he said. "I couldn't find the Realtor. That person should be fired, if you ask me."

"That's too bad. But I think we'll poke around anyway. Ambrose has never seen the inside."

"I told you, you're wasting your time. But suit yourself." He gave a brusque wave. "Good day, Miss DuBois. Mr. Jackson."

He strode up and over to his Rolls while I hovered protectively by the *For Sale* sign. I stayed there until he fired up the car and drove off the property.

"That's not good," Ambrose said, once he'd left.

"Tell me about it. If he wants to turn this place into another hotel, we're doomed."

"Don't jump the gun, Missy. I haven't even seen the inside yet."

Which was true enough. I finally abandoned my post and headed for the front door. Apparently Mr. Solomon hadn't bothered to shut the thing properly, and it stood open a half inch.

I shouldn't, should I? Somehow I "can't-never-could" resist the lure of an open door, and my eyes widened at the thought of all those secrets begging to be discovered. Begging, I tell you. My hand reached for the doorknob.

"Why don't we knock?" It was Ambrose, standing behind me.

Leave it to him to always do the right thing. "You heard him . . . the real estate agent's gone. We could always peek around a little before she comes back. Doesn't cost nuthin' to look."

"Seems to me—"

I gave in to temptation before Ambrose could finish his sentence and pushed open the door. Like before, sunlight glanced off the hardwoods and made them shine like still water on a bayou.

Ambrose whistled. "Look at that. Mahogany."

"That's nothin'. Follow me."

I tiptoed into the foyer as quiet as a church mouse. I didn't mean to intrude, but I wanted to gauge Ambrose's reaction to all of that glorious wood paneling.

"Wow!" He turned 'round and 'round like a little boy in a fun house. "This is something."

"I knew you'd like it."

"Look at that crown molding. That's at least four inches thick."

"You haven't seen anything yet. C'mon." Since Ruby could emerge from the shadows at any minute and cut her eyes at me, I hustled Ambrose through the foyer and into the dining room. Here the wallpaper bloomed with fading magnolias, and chipped dinner plates adorned an antique dining table.

"See what I mean? All it needs is a little work to put it right again. And look out there." I pointed to the kitchen garden, like Mellette had done.

"What's that?"

"A studio," I said. "Can you imagine me out there working on my hats? Think about it, Bo. I could turn it into a showroom and you could have this dining room. We wouldn't have to write rent checks anymore."

"It's something to think about." He glanced nervously toward the foyer. "Maybe we should come back later. I have lots of questions for the Realtor. And then she can show us the second floor."

"Okay, if you say so." He was right, although I hated to admit it. "Let's take a peek at the studio on our way out, though."

We retraced our steps through the foyer, Ambrose's head still swiveling around like a child in a fun house. I let him walk ahead of me and made sure to close the front door extra-tight on the way out. Wouldn't want someone to wander in off the street and traipse through the house all willy-nilly now, would we?

A pea-gravel path led around the house to the garden. By this time, sunshine kissed the Doric columns out back, and a chorus of cicadas practiced trills from inside an overgrown rosebush. We followed the path until it ended at the shed's Dutch door.

"This is where you'd work, huh?" Ambrose asked.

The door's top half stood open, so I peeked over his shoulder to get a glimpse inside.

On the opposite wall sat a rusty metal shelf filled with broken pots, a few trowels, and leftover bags of fertilizer. A pile of towels or rags lay beneath a small window. The room seemed just large enough for a sturdy worktable and my collection of antique hat blocks, not to mention a display rack or two for my finished creations.

"It's perfect," I said.

Tiny motes of dust swooped and swirled through the light of the window like drips falling from a garden hose.

"Looks to be about the right size." Ambrose inched open the door's lower half. "We could even put an awning between this cottage and the house for people to walk back and forth between our two studios."

I quickly moved around him and stepped into the cottage. The minute I entered, though, I noticed something unusual: the smell. Not a normal garden smell like mold or compost or rotting leaves . . . the room smelled like mint. A chemically mint odor, like the kind they used in menthol cigarettes.

I glanced around for the source. The pile I'd spied beneath the window turned out to be a rumpled green business suit and matching shoes.

It was Mellette Babineaux. Her feet splayed out at unnatural angles and her unseeing eyes stared straight ahead. My scream tore through the small space.

"Missy!" Ambrose rushed forward. "Call 9-1-1. Quick!"

But I couldn't move. My feet had become rooted to the ground. Several seconds—or were they minutes?—passed.

"Now!" he said.

That woke me. I whipped out my cell and dialed 9-1-1.

A voice answered before the second ring. "This is 9-1-1. What's your emergency?"

"There's been an accident at the old Sweetwater mansion. Not inside, but outside. We're in a shed. Come quick!"

"Slow down, ma'am." The woman sounded much too calm. "What's the address?"

"I don't know." A flash of memory brought me back to my conversation with Herbert Solomon, though. We'd stood on the front lawn not more than half an hour ago. "It's down the road from Morningside Plantation. That's the one they turned into a big hotel."

The dispatcher was silent, and then she rattled off an address for me to verify.

"That sounds about right," I said.

"And just who are you?"

"Missy DuBois. The gal is the real estate agent here."

"Is she breathing?"

I gasped. "Lord, I hope so."

"Are you with the victim right now?"

Victim? I hadn't really thought about her as a victim. All I knew was that Mellette Babineaux—the one who'd toured me around the house not more than an hour ago—now lay puddled in a heap on a dirty cement floor. "Yes."

"I'm sending help. Keep your phone on you, you hear? Someone may call you back." With that, the line went dead.

I spun around. "They're coming."

"Good," Ambrose said. "Wait for them in the main house. It'll make it easier for them to find us."

I rushed to the Dutch door, anxious to put the sight of the limp body behind me. Quickly, I stumbled over the threshold and hurried down the gravel path.

All sound had disappeared. A cicada probably called to me from its rosebush as I ran by, and my heels no doubt churned through the pea gravel, but I heard none of it. The back door quietly swept open, my shoes floated over the hardwood floor, and I landed in the kitchen.

I paused to catch my breath. Truth be told, I was happy to leave the cottage. At least here I didn't have to look at Mellette and her ashen face. Her legs splayed at unnatural angles. And dear Ambrose trying to keep his composure while my screams woke the dead two states away.

Since I still couldn't breathe, I began to look around as I gulped in air. Above my head hung a pendant light with a hammered copper shade, its soft light illuminating a soapstone counter. Next to that was a farmhouse sink surrounded by a backsplash with dozens of tiny, rose-colored tiles. Maybe if I focused on something else, I could catch my breath. I began to count the tiles from top to bottom. On the thirty-fifth tile, or thereabouts, a siren finally wailed in the distance.

Twelve more tiles and a police car arrived. Staccato bursts of light popped through the kitchen window in candy-cane colors when the cruiser pulled into the driveway. Someone opened and closed a car door before footsteps sounded on the stoop outside.

"In here," I yelled at the top of my lungs, still weak-kneed from our discovery.

A man in a navy uniform appeared on the other side of the screen door. Short and Hispanic, he wore a crew cut and mirrored sunglasses. "Did you call?" He motioned to someone behind him, and I heard footsteps on the gravel path that led to the shed.

He looked like a teenager—all chubby caramel cheeks and black hair. Too young to be a police officer, let alone to carry a sidearm.

"Yes, it was me." I pulled the cell out of my pocket and laid it on the counter. "I used my cell phone."

The officer entered the kitchen and whisked off his sunglasses. "Officer Hernandez. Second district. What's up?"

"My friend and I found someone in the shed outside not more than five minutes ago."

The officer pulled a notepad from his pocket, where I fully expected to see race cars doodled on the cover but, thankfully, it was blank. "Do you know the person?"

I nodded. "Yes. We went to college together a long time ago. Her name's Mellette Babineaux, and she's the Realtor for the property."

When he didn't react, I could tell he didn't know Mellette. Instead, he continued to jot notes while he carefully studied my face.

Someone explained to me once why policemen watched their witnesses so carefully while they spoke. Apparently if a witness glanced left, the officer knew she was relying on memory. But look right and it meant the person was lying. I purposefully stared straight ahead since I had nothing to worry about.

"I wanted to show my friend the studio out back," I said. "That's where we found her."

More writing on his part. "I know. Dispatch told us that, so my partner is out there now. We'll start with that area and establish the chain of custody."

I nodded again. That was a term I was very familiar with, since I'd taken a couple of classes in police procedures as an undergrad at Vanderbilt. At one time I actually toyed with the idea of law school, until I took those classes and realized I'd rather spend my time with sketch pads than cops' notebooks or legal briefs.

"Did you see anything else unusual?" He finally lowered his gaze from my face.

"Now that you mention it, I did." Hadn't I been surprised to see Herbert Solomon's Rolls-Royce hulking outside the house earlier? The man lived in Baton Rouge, after all, which was almost two hours away. He didn't say anything about having an appointment with a real estate agent and that seemed a little strange.

"We ran into Herbert Solomon when we got here," I said.

Even though he hadn't met Mellette, odds were good he'd know about Louisiana's most famous billionaire.

"I've heard of 'im. So he was here too. Coming or going?"

"Going. Told me he couldn't find the Realtor here. Didn't even know if it was a guy or a gal."

"Did he seem upset?"

I thought back to our meeting on the lawn. "More mad than upset. I assumed he wanted to buy this place, only he couldn't find anyone to talk to."

"Anyone with him?"

"No, that was it. But I did meet someone else on my first visit."

He squinted up at me. "First visit?"

"I'm interested in buying this place too. But I had to drag my friend along so he could see it for himself."

"So you met someone else then?"

"Sure enough . . . a caretaker by the name of Ruby," I said. "Don't think she liked me, though."

"Why's that?"

I shrugged. "Apparently it's bad voodoo to visit someone around here first thing on a Monday morning. If you're a woman, anyway. I'd never heard that before."

"You're not from around here, are you?" Officer Hernandez seemed surprised—or was he amused?—by my ignorance.

"No. I moved to town about a year and a half ago. I live down the road. Didn't even know the mansion was for sale until this morning."

"Tell me more about the caretaker."

"There's not a whole lot to say. She seemed to think they did voodoo ceremonies around here a while ago, or some-such thing. Said something about amulets and charms. Does that mean any-thing?"

Now it was his turn to shrug. "It could. We get strange stuff out here. Think that's enough for now. You'll be free to go in a minute."

"But aren't you going to ask me to come back with you to the sta-tion so you can write up my statement?" That's how they explained it back in those classes at Vanderbilt.

"Definitely. But we have to wrap up things here first. Get our re-port to Investigative Support Services. You can go, though. Do you have a ride home?"

"I drove over with my friend." That's when I remembered Ambrose. Poor thing was still trapped in the shed with Mellette's limp body and a police officer. "I'd better go find him."

I hastily said good-bye to the officer and stepped through the kitchen door. Somehow the sky seemed darker now than when we first arrived. I tiptoed along the garden path and met up with Ambrose about halfway down.

"Hi, Bo. Did they ask you a lot of questions too?"

"Sure did." Ambrose looked drained. "The guy seemed surprised I didn't know the lady lying on the floor next to me. Once he got past that, though, he said I could go. Said something about you and me heading over to the police station later."

I nodded. "I know. By the way, was she—"

"Yes. She's dead." Ambrose stopped in the middle of the path, his eyes haunted. "But there's something else, Missy."

"What is it?"

"I saw something back there in the shed. Something strange."

I laid my hand on his shoulder. "We found a dead body, Bo. Of course you saw something strange."

"No, it's not that." He shrugged my hand away. Whatever he'd seen, it'd shaken him to the core.

"Tell me. What's wrong?"

"Somebody left a cross back there. A black cross."

"Why would they do that?"

"I don't know. But there's more."

How could there be more? Already my legs felt like muscadine jelly, and I longed to sit on a garden bench or a backyard swing or even an overturned bucket.

"There was something on the cross. Looked like blood to me. Fresh blood too."

"But that would mean . . ." I couldn't finish the sentence.

"Yeah. They must have killed her right before we got here."

I sagged forward, suddenly winded. Thankfully Ambrose caught me and steadied me against his chest. Why, oh why, did we ever come back to the Sweetwater mansion?

We remained like that for several minutes, each of us lost in thought. Finally, some feeling returned to my legs, and I straightened.

"Whatever we do, Bo, we've got to find out what happened. Mellette Babineaux and I went to college together. Same sorority and everything."

"Okay." His eyes narrowed. "But you have to promise me you won't go running off by yourself. I don't want you to get hurt."

"I promise." I raised my hand in the Boy Scout salute to prove it.

"The only question is . . . where do we start?"

"My granddaddy always said it's best to start at the beginning and keep going 'til you get to the end."

Of course, my dear granddaddy stole that line from a famous picture book about a girl and a white rabbit, but that was neither here nor there at this point. Somehow, Ambrose and I had landed smack-dab in the middle of another crime scene. Time would only tell if we'd stumbled down a rabbit hole of our own.

Chapter 3

Once we finished up at the police station, Ambrose and I were free to go. We drove away in his Audi and soon pulled up to our rent house, where a bramble of butterflies met us at the garden gate and a half-eaten sack of beignets still sat on the kitchen table.

After entering the room, I wandered to the sink and began to rinse a coffee mug. My heart wasn't in it, though, and I sensed Ambrose when he walked up behind me.

"You're going to scrub that cup to a nub," he whispered over my shoulder.

Which was true enough. "I know, but I can't figure out what to do next. It's like I want to know what happened back at Sweetwater, but I don't."

"Tell you what." He took hold of my shoulders and twisted me around until I faced him. "You let that dish alone. Go on down to your shop and get some work done. It'll be a sight more productive than moping around here."

Of course, he was right. "But what about you? I hate to leave you after everything that happened to us this morning."

He waved away my concern. "I'll be fine. I'm going to answer a few e-mails and then straighten out my bookings for the week. We can meet up later at the Factory."

"If you insist."

The Factory was our nickname for the shopping center where we both kept studios. Even though the developers labeled it the Pepper Palace, since it was once a spice factory, no one ever called it by its given name.

I glanced around the quiet kitchen, searching for my car keys. Like it or not, standing at the kitchen sink and worrying a coffee mug to death wasn't going to do anyone a lick of good. After spotting them by the unread mail, I dropped the keys into my pocket. "Call me if you hear anything. Anything at all. Especially from those police officers."

He rolled his eyes, which I pretended not to notice as I left the kitchen and made my way to the car.

Thank goodness Sweetwater lay in the opposite direction from the Factory. I hopped into my VW bug—which I'd named Ringo, since it *was* a Beetle—and pulled onto the highway. After a moment, I drove by a sugarcane field, where row upon row of chubby plant stalks grew knee-high on their way to a September harvest.

Another mile or so and my view changed. Now a Union Carbide plant burped steam high in the air, its bright silver tubes scaffolding the furnace stacks. The end stack always reminded me of a giant birthday candle with a hot orange flame that licked the sky.

At this point, everything around looked slick and shiny. Especially since midday sun ricocheted off all of the metal and glanced through Ringo's windshield.

No wonder my shirt collar felt damp. Fortunately, the turnoff for Highway 18 appeared after a moment.

Two more miles and I arrived at the Factory. Hallelujah, someone had saved the ancient building from the wrecking ball and converted it to a "shopping and dining destination." With weathered bricks on the outside and original wide-plank floors on the inside, the Pepper Palace was now a showplace for brides and grooms. Crowning Glory lay on the ground floor, next to Ambrose's Allure Couture, Brooke's Bridal Portraits, and Flowers by Dana.

All of us catered to brides in one way or another. One of my favorites—outside of Ambrose's studio, of course—was Pink Cake Boxes, on the second floor. And not just because the baker passed out samples every Tuesday and Friday afternoon between 1:30 and 2:00, mind you.

I drove into the parking lot and pulled up alongside my assistant's battered pickup. I'd first met Beatrice when she worked as a tour guide at Morningside Plantation. That was before Herbert Solomon bought the place and fired its staff lock, stock, and barrel.

Usually I found Bea organizing receipts by the cash register, and today was no exception. She glanced up when I walked through the door, an enormous pair of rhinestone earrings brushing the collar of her Carhartt work shirt. That was Beatrice . . . hard and soft. Iron-wood denim and sparkly jewels. A rusty Ford pickup she'd painted bubblegum pink.

"Hey, I didn't expect you to come in today," she said.

"I know. I was gonna take the day off. But you wouldn't believe the morning I've had."

"What happened?" She patted the stool next to her.

I dropped my purse behind the counter and slid onto the stool. "It all started when Ambrose got a hankering for beignets." Amazing to think that such an innocent craving could lead to so much drama. "Only instead of going to the bakery, I stopped by the Sweetwater mansion."

She tilted her head. "I heard that one's for sale now."

"Yeah." Although, by now, that was beside the point.

"My uncle told me about it. Said it's a shame no one in the family wants it."

"That's right. I forgot your uncle sells real estate." Beatrice had once tacked a calendar in our break room that had his picture splashed across the front. He wore an amazingly gaudy shirt in the photo that was hard to forget.

"I wanted Ambrose to see the house," I said. "But we found Mellette Babineaux in the cottage out back. I'm afraid she was dead."

Beatrice's hand flew to her mouth. "You can't be serious." She whispered the words through her fingertips. "Are you sure?"

I nodded gently. " 'Fraid so."

"What happened?"

"I called 9-1-1 and got some police officers down there. They took over, so I really don't know after that. Her body was all twisted, though, and her face looked gray, like someone had tried to polish it with silver cleaner. Strangest thing I've ever seen."

"Gray, huh?" Beatrice studied the floorboards beneath us while we spoke.

"Yep, that's what it looked like to me."

"Light gray or dark gray?"

I was about to shrug when I remembered why Beatrice might ask that. She'd once studied chemistry at LSU. Until she read *Pharmaceutical Analysis* and decided she'd rather die than memorize API structures. She'd know what to make of Mellette's skin coloring.

"Light gray. Ashy."

"Sounds like someone poisoned her." She finally glanced up. "Probably one of the acids."

"Could be. I didn't see any wounds. And no one knows how long she'd been lying there."

"I still can't believe it," she said. "Who'd do that? I worked for Miss Babineaux one summer when she and my uncle were partners. Such a great lady. Can't imagine someone would want to kill her."

"I thought she seemed nice too, when I met her this morning. We're sorority sisters, you know. She went to Vanderbilt a few years before me. It doesn't make sense."

Mellette and I had chatted about our time in college only a few hours before. We'd stood on those beautiful hardwood floors, which looked like still water beneath my feet, next to an enormous tapestry of herons two-stepping somewhere in the Gulf. I could almost taste the sweet tea Ruby had brought me.

"Say, I met someone else. The caretaker. She got me some tea. But, boy, did she give me the heebie-jeebies."

"You must mean Ruby. She's been there forever. And I know what you're saying about creepy. She lives out back on the bayou . . . so there you go."

My eyes widened. "Do people really live out there?"

"Heck, yeah. A bunch of people. All around the Atchafalaya River, where Miss Ruby comes from."

The last time I saw her, Ruby had watched Mellette and me from by the staircase. There was no telling what she'd seen or heard since then.

"Think I should go talk to her?" I asked. "She might know what happened this morning, and the police didn't seem interested in her when I brought her up."

"You?" Beatrice began to chuckle, but she stopped when she saw my face. "Missy, I don't mean to disrespect you, but it's kinda wild on the river. You can't go out there in high heels and expect anyone to take you seriously."

"Why not? I'm sure I can manage." I tried to not sound hurt, even though my pride had been wounded for the second time in one day. Sounded like no one was interested in finding out what had happened to my sorority sister, and that struck me as downright shameful.

"Most people paddle a pirogue out there. Do you even know what that is?"

"A *pir*-what?" I'd never heard the term before.

"It's a boat. A long, narrow one. Please tell me you've seen a picture somewhere."

"Can't say that I have. How do I get one?" My stubborn side had kicked in, and now I was determined to speak with the gal from this morning.

"Well, they rent 'em out to people who hunt for wood ducks and deer. But then they'll want to give you a full tour. Course, you can always borrow one. My uncle has one. He bought it so he could figure out the property lines around here."

"Think he'd loan it to me?"

"You're serious?" she asked. "You want to float the Atchafalaya and find Miss Ruby?"

I drew back my shoulders so at least I'd look confident. "Yes. Yes, I do."

"Okay, then. I'll ask him. He's got a flatback with a motor, so you wouldn't even have to paddle."

"Whatever you say." Truth be told, I knew as much about a flatback or a pirogue as I did about a wood duck. "I could use a tour guide, though. Wanna help me?"

Now it was her turn to look surprised. "Me? But then who'll watch the shop?"

"You let me worry about that. I'll forward the calls to my cell—" I paused. For some reason, the pocket that usually held my cell felt unusually light. I patted the material, which lay flat against my leg. Empty as a drum.

And then I remembered: the kitchen at Sweetwater. I'd tossed the phone onto the counter once the police officer arrived.

"Sugar!" I said. "I must have left my cell at Sweetwater." No matter . . . I could always get it later. "Right now you call your uncle while I put a note up in the window. We don't have any appointments this afternoon. I already checked. Let's get out of here before I change my mind."

Next thing I knew, Beatrice and I had arrived at her uncle's house. The turn-of-the-century cottage had a pitched, shingled roof, baskets of flowers hanging over the front porch, and a lush side garden. A wood canoe sat on blocks in the driveway.

I parked Ringo and we both walked over to it. The seats were made of white oak slats and a five-horsepower Honda motor perched at the very end.

"How do you suppose we get it in the water?" I asked.

"My uncle will help us. No way we can carry it with that motor."

Just then, a man emerged from the house and joined us. He wore a different shirt than the one I'd seen in the calendar—praise the Lord—but I'd recognize him anywhere.

Deeply tanned, with a square jaw and thick black hair, he was handsome in a rugged kind of way.

"Hey, Beatrice." He gathered his niece in a bear hug.

"Uncle Hank," Beatrice squeaked. "This here is my boss, Missy DuBois. The one I told you about."

"Course. Of course." He finally let go of Beatrice and stuck out his hand. "I've heard all about you and your store. Don't worry, it's all good."

I shook his hand, which felt surprisingly rough. "Well, that's nice to hear." I thought Realtors spent their days inside, typing contracts or filing folders or whatnot, but this man's hand was as tough as an alligator's back.

"Bea here says you want to go on the bayou this morning. Good day for it. Wind's down and the weather's tolerable." He pointed at the pirogue. "Let me give you a lesson."

Beatrice stepped in front of him. "That's okay, Uncle. I'll steer, so she doesn't have to. We're headed out to Miss Ruby's, about three miles in, from what I could see on the parish assessor's website."

He beamed. "This one here's quite the detective. We used to give her MoonPies, back when she was a little thing, for digging up records at the county courthouse. 'Til she outgrew her blue jeans. Ain't that right, Bea?"

Beatrice's face immediately pinked, so I jumped in to save her. "Thank you for loaning us the boat, Mr. Dupre. We only need it for a few hours. And Beatrice here told me all about how she used to work for you. I believe she said you and Mellette Babineaux were partners once."

The smile slipped down his face. He'd apparently heard about the murder at Sweetwater. Not that I was surprised, since news traveled fast around these small towns. Or, as my granddaddy would say, "It flies at the speed of boredom."

"Terrible tragedy," I said. "I'm so sorry for your loss."

"Yes. Yes, it was."

"My friend and I were the ones who found her, you know."

He gave a tight nod. "So I'd heard. Can't believe she's gone. My phone's been ringing off the hook. Guess everyone wants to be first in line to tell me."

"But that won't happen." Beatrice gave his shoulder a comforting pat. "My uncle has a police scanner, so he hears everything first."

"You don't say."

He and Beatrice exchanged quick looks that were hard to read. "If you don't mind my asking," he asked, "what were *you* doing down there this morning?"

"I don't mind at all. I thought I'd take a look around Sweetwater since it's for sale. Guess I couldn't resist."

That seemed to perk him up a bit. "What do you know? Did you get a chance to see the whole property?"

"I did, but not my friend."

"The house is beautiful. And priced to sell too."

"You don't have to convince me, Mr. Dupre."

He reached into the pocket of his khakis. "Maybe I can help you out." He withdrew a shiny business card that had the same picture he'd used for the calendar. "Here's my card, in case you have questions about the property."

I flinched, so he quickly spoke again. "Not now, of course. But once the dust settles. I'm not hard to get ahold of."

Funny that he didn't seem saddened by the news about Mellette Babineaux. At least not enough to put aside his business. "Thank you—um—kindly." I took the card. "We'll have the boat back to you as soon as we can."

"No rush. Gotta go to work, so there won't be any fishing for me. Let's get it in your truck, Bea. Grab that end."

Together, Beatrice and her uncle hoisted the pirogue up and over the tailgate of her pickup. When they finished, they both climbed into the front seat while I settled into the back.

Air rushed through the open windows as soon as we reached the highway. I couldn't quite catch the conversation up front, but it seemed to involve Sweetwater. I heard the word *gris-gris*, which someone had told me were good-luck charms, and *wangas*, which I guessed were the bad ones.

Several miles passed—during which time my neck developed an

awful crick from leaning forward—until the river appeared. Stands of tupelo cypress rose from the soupy water like celery stalks half submerged.

After a few more minutes on Highway 975, we reached a dirt road, which looked like all of the other dirt roads we'd passed. Then Beatrice made a hard right and we jerked to a stop at a boat landing.

Here the cypress parted naturally. When I hopped out of the pickup, I landed smack-dab in some wet clay that oozed around my favorite strappy sandals. My heart sank when I saw the mess.

"It'll wash off." Beatrice stuck her head through the driver's-side window. "Don't worry." When she swung open the car door and jumped out, I saw that she'd worn ballet flats with her work shirt. *Smart girl.*

I jerked up my foot and scouted the horizon. Straight ahead of us, thick mats of sphagnum moss floated on the water. A wall of humidity pressed against me and sucked the breath from my lungs. Maybe this wasn't such a good idea, after all.

"C'mon, Missy," Beatrice said. "Get yourself some skeeter juice and a cap from the truck. We'll get this thing in the water."

I yanked my other heel from the mud and retreated to the pickup. Once I'd doused myself with Off, I twisted my hair into a makeshift bun and tucked it under a faded LSU ball cap. Surely Ambrose would laugh if he saw me, but thank goodness he was miles away at our rent house.

By the time I'd finished, Beatrice and her uncle had lowered the pirogue in the river. I duckwalked over to them and climbed into the boat. Beatrice followed me, only she sat next to the motor and placed her hand on the boat's tiller. With a big push from her uncle, we sailed away.

"I'll take your truck back, Bea," he called out. "Phone me when you want a ride."

"Thank you!"

The launch began to recede as we floated away. After a minute, Hank Dupre was no bigger than a splotch of mud on my sandal. When he disappeared altogether, Beatrice started the motor, and the sound split the quiet air.

We roared past beds of hydrilla and clumps of cattails as tall as Ambrose. Above us flew swallowtail kites that scoured the trees for lizards and katydids. The smell of rotting leaves, decaying roots, and mold engulfed us, reminding me of the time I left a houseplant too long on the windowsill.

After a bit, Beatrice cut the motor and the air fell quiet again. Now the sounds of the swamp engulfed us. A pair of little blue herons cawed back and forth beside us, a spoonbill's massive wings beat the air above, and an osprey splashed the water somewhere, no doubt looking for lunch.

"Beautiful, isn't it?" Beatrice whispered.

I spun around. "Gorgeous. You seem to know your way around here."

"Used to come out with my uncle. We'd dip our nets over the side for crawfish."

"How fun! Maybe Ambrose and I should try it sometime."

She arched an eyebrow. "Gotta warn you . . . the fishing gets pretty messy. Even waders won't keep the mud out. Lots of crawfish, though. That and largemouth bass. Some folks around here don't ever go to the grocery store. Everything they need is right here on the river."

I watched the wake behind us, which stretched for yards and yards. "Speaking of which . . . how close are we to Ruby's house?"

"Should be up ahead."

I twisted back around. After a few more minutes, a ramshackle camp appeared that had two rusty mobile homes. Looked like singlewides to me, with cinder blocks placed beneath them to raise them from the muck. At the foot of the trailers was a listing dock.

The home on the left looked especially quirky. A statue of the Virgin Mary presided over a purple grotto at that one; its plaster shaped like an open clamshell.

"That's it." Beatrice grabbed an oar from under her seat. "The one on the left."

Of course. I followed Beatrice's lead and grabbed the paddle under my seat. By now I'd moved past glistening and had begun to sweat, so what harm could a little rowing do?

Together we steered the pirogue to the dock. When we reached it, Beatrice grabbed a rope and twisted it into a hitch, which she looped onto the dock's scratched cleat.

She hopped out of the boat after that. "See, that wasn't so bad."

I heaved myself up and out after her. "True enough. Though these sandals are going to be the death of me yet."

When the dock swayed underfoot, I worried I might tumble into the muck and disappear forever. But only for an instant. Because now I faced another—more pressing—problem.

A spotted mongrel had appeared on the dock. Clearly not the welcoming committee.

Beatrice noticed it too. "They're usually friendly." Her voice faltered.

"He doesn't look too friendly to me."

"It's okay, boy." Her words came out in a singsong. "We won't hurt you."

"I don't think that's what it's worried about, Bea."

Call it instinct or call it foolishness, but I'd rather make the first move in times like these. So I shoved my fists against my hips and worked up a respectable growl that began in the back of my throat and rumbled through my lips. Hallelujah, the dog wasn't deaf, because it grudgingly sank back on its haunches.

A moment later, a screen door banged open behind us.

"Whatcha doin' out here?"

Ruby was standing in the doorway of the trailer. She wore the same silver ponytail and wary expression I'd seen earlier.

"*Tais-toi*, Jack," she yelled at the dog.

"We wanted to say hello." I gingerly moved around the dog and walked to where she stood. "Remember me? You were nice enough to get me some sweet tea this morning."

She eyed me warily. "I knows why yer here. Yer here about Miss Babineaux. Dey tole me she's dead."

So much for pleasantries. Although I had to admire her straightforwardness, since that was exactly why we'd come.

"Yes, she died this morning," I said. "God rest her soul. I brought my assistant, Beatrice, out here with me."

"All right, den. Da moustiques gonna eat us alive if'n we don' go in." She motioned for us to follow her into the ramshackle home.

The rooms we entered were dark and cluttered. All along the wall of the living room hung crosses of various shapes and sizes, of all things. Just like the cross Ambrose had told me about this morning.

They hung in groups of twos and threes above an old-fashioned television set, while dozens more decorated a thin wall that separated the area from the kitchen. I couldn't see any rhyme or reason to their placement, since fancy ones dressed in plastic rosettes and sequins hung right next to rough-hewn ones made from kindling.

Never in my life had I seen so many crosses, and I grew up going to church, after all.

"Such an interesting collection you have." I glanced around the trailer. The only place to sit was a plaid couch covered in plastic, but that was strewn with yellowed copies of the *Times-Picayune* and Dollar General plastic bags. What choice did I have but to lean against the flimsy wall, crosses and all?

"Dey ward off da evil," Ruby said.

I tried to be casual, even though I worried I might crash right through the wall and land in the kitchen on my backside. "That's what we've come to talk to you about. My friend found a cross this morning, out there in the shed at Sweetwater. Do you know anything about it?"

"Dat's why ya be here? Ya tink I had somethin' ta do wit da murder?"

"No, no. I'm not saying that." While I don't hold to lying, this seemed a fine time for a little fib. "Of course, we don't think you had *anything* to do with it. Nothing at all. We need your help, though."

"Mah help? Whatcha be talkin' 'bout? I don' know nutin' 'bout what happened. Told da policeman da same ting."

Casually, I waved my hand around. "But you know this area. And the people who live around here. Was anyone mad at Miss Babineaux?"

Ruby's bony shoulders shrugged. "Could be. Lotsa people put da curses on."

"But did *you* hear anything?" I asked. "Maybe someone threaten her?"

"Folks don' like wot she be doin' wit' da land. Tryin' to get us to move off the river. Gah-lee, dat's all we got."

She spoke so quickly, it took me a moment to decipher her words. "I see. But would that be reason enough for someone to kill her?"

"All we gots is de land 'round here," she repeated. "Firs' be da French wot comes, den da Canadiens. Now you got folks swarm 'round here like da moustiques. Wot's left? Maybe dat's why she ain't got no friends. None of us be goin' ta dat funeral, right Hollis?"

She jerked her head sideways, toward the kitchen. She'd aimed her words at a figure who sat at a plastic dinette set. It was a pale boy, about sixteen, dressed in a dirty sleeveless T-shirt and Nike running shorts.

"No, ma'am," he said.

"Dat be ma grandson." She motioned for him to come forward. He had the same wide-set eyes and broad forehead as his grandmother. "He done keep me company in ma old age."

"Nice to meet you," I said. "My name's Missy and this is Beatrice."

He ducked his head shyly. "Nice to meet ya. Hope old Jack didn't bother you none."

"You heard that, huh?" I smiled. "Turns out neither of us likes to hear growling. You go to school around here?"

"No, ma'am. Kinda doin' it on ma own."

Funny, but I hadn't noticed any textbooks lying around the trailer. About the closest thing were the old newspapers covering the couch. Not to mention Internet coverage was probably spotty in these parts.

"Interesting. We just came by to ask your grandmother some questions." I turned to face Ruby. "What about this morning? Did you notice anything strange around the mansion?"

"Hard ta say. Ah left early."

"Do you remember when?" Beatrice asked. She'd been so quiet, I'd forgotten she was there.

"Nah. But I saw you," She jerked her thumb at me. "And dat young feller too."

"So you saw—" I didn't finish the sentence. Ruby must have seen Ambrose, which meant she was still at Sweetwater when I brought Bo over.

Such an interesting visit this had turned out to be. "Well, we won't take up any more of your time," I said. "We all feel terrible about what happened."

I reached for the screen door, but Ruby grabbed my hand before I could open it. She thrust something into my palm and then curled my fingers around it.

"Here. Take dis." Her eyes bore into mine. "Don' go nowhere witout it. Nowhere."

"Um, thank you." It was a pouch, and the material scratched my palm. "So nice to see you again. And nice to meet you, Hollis."

I nodded vaguely at the boy before pushing the screen door open. It swayed open with a loud screech, but the noise faded as I made my way down the stairs and across the dock. Thankfully, Jack, the mongrel, was gone, so I had a clear shot to the pirogue.

I finally paused when I reached it.

"What was that all about?" Beatrice had caught up to me and stood peering over my shoulder.

I shrugged and then uncurled my fingers to expose the pouch. Its red flannel had been cinched with a silk ribbon, which I carefully loosened. When I tipped the bag over into my other hand, two dried bones—chicken, thankfully—tumbled out. Next came a gray pebble and something green and spiky that looked familiar. I took a whiff. Sure enough . . . catnip.

Beatrice sucked in her breath. "Wow. She gave you a gris-gris. That means she likes you."

"You're kidding."

"Trust me. She doesn't want anything bad to happen to you." She moved away and then lowered herself into the boat.

Didn't that just beat all. For one thing, I'd never seen so many crosses in one place; more than a monk would have. She'd also talked about Ambrose, which meant she must have been at Sweetwater during the murder. And finally . . . what was she trying to protect me from?

Although it was hotter than a Dutch oven out on the dock, I couldn't help but shudder.

Chapter 4

For the second time that day, I returned to the rent house with something in my hand. Only this time it was something far more interesting than a sack of greasy beignets.

"Whatcha got there?" Ambrose noticed the treasure as soon as I walked into the kitchen, its walls warmed by the late-afternoon sun.

"A gift. From the caretaker I told you about at Sweetwater."

Too many hours had passed since I'd last seen him. He was back at the kitchen table, only now he held a newspaper in his hand instead of a fork and knife. At some point, he must've gone back to his studio, though, because I spotted tailor's chalk on his fingers.

I'd tried to return to work too, after my float trip down the river with Beatrice. But I couldn't concentrate, so I ended up signing a few checks and calling a few clients before I called it quits and came home.

"What kind of gift?" He eyed the pouch curiously.

"She gave me a gris-gris. Have you ever heard of such a thing in your life?"

"Of course I have. I went to Auburn, remember? Spent lots of weekends in New Orleans."

Carefully, I placed the bag on the table. "That's right. Well, Beatrice and I visited the caretaker's home today. I got to paddle a pirogue and everything."

"Good for you."

"We went to see her because she was at Sweetwater this morning." I plopped beside him and once again loosened the bag's tie. "You won't believe where she lives."

"Do tell."

"On the bayou, in this old mobile home. Place looks like it's been flooded ten times over."

"Didn't you say she's about eighty?"

"At least. She lives out there with her grandson. And I saw the craziest thing at her place." The bag finally opened, so I turned over the pouch and the contents spilled out.

He shot me a curious look.

"There were crosses at her place, Bo. Dozens and dozens of crosses. Big ones, little ones, and everything in between."

"Maybe the old lady likes crosses." Ambrose reached for the chicken bones, which were tied together with a piece of leather. He turned them thoughtfully between his fingers.

"True. But you also found a cross next to Mellette's body this morning."

"I remember. But what if she's just really devout? Even the voodoo around here has some Roman Catholic in it, you know."

"That would explain the Virgin Mary in her front yard. But there's more."

"More?" Once he'd finished with the bones, Ambrose began to toy with the pebble, which was crisscrossed by veins of quartz.

"She said she saw you too. That would mean she was at Sweetwater when we found the body this morning."

"Bottom line is you think she had something to do with the real estate agent's murder. Is that what you're saying?"

"Looks like it," I said. "Why else would she say that? Plus, there was no love lost between her and Mellette Babineaux. She got really angry this morning when Mellette made her get me some sweet tea."

"Yeah, but it's a big jump from being angry at someone to actually killing them."

Leave to it Ambrose to be rational, even with a pile of voodoo tokens in front of him.

"But it does happen. And remember, the murder scene was pretty tidy. Which means the killer probably knew the victim. That's what they say, anyway." Of course, the "they" I was referring to happened to be found in textbooks I'd read at least ten years before, but he didn't need to know that.

"I suppose. What do you want to do now?" He pulled the last item from the bag: the catnip. "Want to go back to the police station?"

"I guess so. By the way, that's catnip, right?"

"Yep."

"So why would she put that in there?"

"It's supposed to make people happy too. Not just cats."

"How would you know such a thing? Wait . . . don't tell me." I held up my hand. "I've had enough craziness for one day."

"So, let's go then. Before the officer from this morning gets off work."

Truth be told, what I *wanted* to do was draw a nice, hot bath and wash my filthy toes, but maybe the police should be told about the crosses.

"Let me change first," I said. "These poor clothes have been through the wringer."

I rose from the bench and headed for the bathroom, desperate to run a washcloth over my feet and ankles. Once done, I tossed on a new shirt and a pair of shorts.

Five minutes later, I returned to the kitchen. "All set. This time I'm not going to let the officer's age throw me for a loop. I know what I saw today, even if he acts like I'm crazy."

Ambrose and I made our way through the living room, where he held open the front door for me. The sun had mellowed, although the air still felt thick enough to drink with a straw.

Halfway to the Audi, I stopped. "I almost forgot. I left my cell back at Sweetwater this morning. Mind if we go and get it?"

"I don't know." His fingers stalled over the passenger-door handle. "The police will have the place roped off. They don't want us there."

"But I need my phone. We might as well get it over with. And I won't touch anything else inside. I promise."

He went back to opening the car door and stepped aside as it swung open. "It's also getting kinda late. Your Officer Hernandez could've gone home by now."

"I know, I know. It's not convenient. But do it for me?" I didn't mean to pout, but somehow my bottom lip jutted out. Thankfully, Ambrose can't-never-could tell me no, and he rolled his eyes.

"Fine. If that's what you want." He went over to his side of the car and dropped into the driver's seat. "Honestly. You do have me trained, don't you?"

"Now don't go saying that, Bo. You're concerned for my welfare. I think it's sweet."

He fumbled with the ignition before firing up the car. "That's a nice way of saying I'm whipped."

"Sweet," I repeated, although he did have a point. I decided then and there to tone down the bossiness, although it was anyone's guess how long *that* would last.

Silence enveloped us as we drove away from the rent house. Thick mats of kudzu rolled by, the ropey vines swallowing everything in their path, from chain-link fences to telephone poles and stop signs.

After a bit, we passed Morningside Plantation—the one owned by Mr. Solomon—which was fronted by a mile of white picket fence. The house resembled a grand wedding cake, with two tiers of sugared columns and a flat roof where someone could plop a porcelain bride and groom.

Ambrose must have enjoyed the view too, because he slowed the car.

Vvvrrrooommm. A driver behind us revved his engine, apparently not sharing our enthusiasm for the mansion next to us. Although Ambrose had picked up the pace, the car soon pulled up alongside us.

"Sugar! They're sure in a hurry," I said.

"That's okay. We'll let 'em pass. Probably on their way to Baton Rouge."

The speeding tires created a funnel of dirt and pea gravel, but I managed to glimpse a Mississippi license plate amid all of the dust. Definitely an out-of-towner with no appreciation for history and a lead foot.

Everything returned to normal after that, and we arrived at Sweetwater within a few minutes. My heart sank when the car came to a stop, though. Yellow Day-Glo caution tape wound in and around the gorgeous old oaks, culminating in a giant X between the two front columns nearest the door. Did it have to be so ugly? Even the ever-present kudzu would have been better than this.

"Now, that's just pitiful," I said.

"So, what do we do?"

"I guess we go to the kitchen."

Although I hadn't mentioned it, I had another reason for wanting to return to Sweetwater: Somehow I felt responsible for it. As if the mansion needed me. Which couldn't have been further from the truth. By this time, at least five generations of messy toddlers and hell-bent kids had careened through the property, not to mention assorted dogs and cats. Even Civil War soldiers had bloodied the dirt with their muskets and gunpowder. But silly or not, I wanted to watch over it.

I climbed out of the Audi and hurried up the lawn. Couldn't they at least have been more careful when they threaded the tape through the columns? Someone had used jagged strips of duct tape at the X's corners, which made them look like silver Band-Aids on a fluorescent dressing.

I paused, and not just because of the catawampus tape, either. We weren't the only ones on the property. Another car sat in the same spot where Herbert Solomon had parked his Rolls-Royce. A dusty car, with Mississippi license plates, of all things.

"Someone's here," I said.

"I can see that." Ambrose joined me on the lawn. "Wonder who it is?"

"I think it's the guy who passed us on the road." I walked beyond the front door and headed around the corner of the house.

Sure enough, someone stood next to a gnarled oak, his lips curled around an electronic cigarette. The guy was in his late twenties, with blond hair shaved at the sides and a lick of it in his eyes. What really surprised me, though, was a chunk of gold that glinted on his right wrist. It was an enormous Rolex that sparkled in the sun. I'd never seen one so large or so shiny.

"Hello, there," I said. Might as well announce myself since it was only a matter of time before he spotted me.

He lowered the cigarette. "Uh, can I help you?"

"That depends. I'm Missy DuBois, from down the road. I think you passed us on the highway."

"Probably. I like to go fast."

"I can tell." I glanced behind him. "Do you know if the police ever came back?"

"No idea. Just got here myself, so I wouldn't know."

By this time, Ambrose had rounded the corner, and he joined us. "Hi. I see you've met Missy. I'm Ambrose Jackson." He held out his hand to the stranger.

"Ashley Cox. I'm the owner here." The guy clicked off the cigarette and pocketed it before shaking Ambrose's hand.

"Really? If you don't mind my saying, you look a little young to own this place," Ambrose said.

He shrugged. "It was my parents'. My brother and I took over their trust when they died."

"That's too bad about your parents," I said. "I'm sorry for your loss."

He tossed off the comment with a wave of his hand. "Yeah, well, it's been a while. I left for college, and then my brother moved out. We didn't come back much after that."

I purposefully softened my tone. "Such a pity. But surely you must have heard about what happened here this morning."

"The police told me. Said something about finding a body at the house. That's all I know."

"It was Mellette Babineaux, your real estate agent. But . . . you must have known her."

He shook his head. "I never met her. Not once. We did everything by text. Same thing, really."

It wasn't the same thing at all, but that was neither here nor there at this point.

"So, where's your brother?" Ambrose asked.

"Beats me. I think he's in Colorado. He wants me to handle this mess, like I handle everything else." The words dripped with sarcasm.

"Hmmm." The conversation had turned a little dark. "Say . . . I went inside your house this morning," I said. "My favorite part—"

"Look." He pulled away from the oak. "I'm sorry, but I don't have a lot of time. The cops want me to check out the house and tell 'em if I see anything different. Hell if I'd know. I haven't been back in ten years."

Ambrose took the hint. "We won't keep you, but we left something inside. Mind if we go get it?"

"Suit yourself. The back doors aren't taped."

We walked to a set of French doors with Ashley leading the way. He pulled a key ring with a Yale crest from his pocket and then jammed a key into the lock.

I walked behind him as the door swung open. Only shapes and shadows were visible in the dim light, but then he flipped on a light switch, and fat magnolias bloomed on the wallpaper. We stood in the dining room, with its exquisite chandelier and antique porcelain.

"You have such gorgeous things." I absentmindedly reached for a teacup on the table until I remembered my promise to Ambrose not to touch anything but my cell phone. My finger recoiled as if the cup was hot.

"These things didn't belong to us," Ashley said. "The real estate agent told me she was gonna bring in a stager. Probably bought all of this stuff at a store around here."

"Really." Somehow that changed everything. Now the china cups didn't look quite so shiny, or the oil painting on the wall so exquisite. In fact, it was probably a poster from the local Hobby Lobby, now that I had a chance to examine it. My eyes flew to the cut-glass chandelier above my head.

"Plastic," he said. "We sold most of my mom's stuff after she passed away."

Ambrose hadn't said a word, although I knew what he was thinking. He was probably wondering why I'd fallen so hard and so fast for a house I knew so little about. Like how the family china probably came from Tuesday Morning, or how the "crystal" chandelier was really plastic.

"Guess it's time to get my cell." I faked a smile. "I'll just pop into the kitchen and get it."

"Here." Ashley reached out to stop me. "Let me go first. All the lights are off."

He darted in front of me and began to walk toward the kitchen. I followed, while Ambrose stayed behind.

At least the kitchen up ahead looked authentic. The heavy soap-stone counter still looked like it'd been there forever. Ditto for the tin ceiling tiles that stretched from one edge of the room to the other. Not to mention the mosaic tiles above the sink, which had given me a welcome distraction while I waited for a police officer.

I spied my cell on the counter. "There it is." Someone—probably Officer Hernandez—had pushed it into the corner.

"Well, there you go."

Casually, I dropped the phone into the pocket of my shorts. "So when did your parents buy this place?"

"They didn't buy it. My grandfather gave it to them for a wedding present. He got it from his dad. Guess we're done in here."

Ashley kept glancing at the doorway to the kitchen as if he couldn't wait to leave. But I was hungry for more information. "Aren't you sorry to see it go? Imagine all the history that took place here."

"I guess. But it's only business."

Cccrrraaassshhh! Before I could say more, something banged in the hall. Something loud and hard and hollow, like a bowling ball falling on a pine alley.

"What the—"

We both sprinted out of the kitchen. I skidded to a stop when I reached the foyer and saw Ambrose leaning over the floor with a rolled-up carpet next to his feet. He held a curved ruler—of all things—in his hand, and he straightened when he saw me.

"Sorry." He sheepishly pocketed the tailor's tool. "Couldn't help myself when I saw the trapdoor. Didn't think it'd slam shut like that."

I glanced down. Although it was dark, four lines appeared in the hardwoods near Ambrose's feet, where someone had carved the trapdoor. "What does it lead to?"

Ambrose didn't answer. And that was when I remembered his admonition not to touch anything. "Ambrose Jackson. I thought we weren't supposed to touch anything. What exactly did you do?"

"Couldn't help myself. And I happened to have my tailor's ruler on me."

"That's no reason—"

"You found it." Ashley's voice was soft.

I wheeled around. "What exactly did he find?"

"The trapdoor leads to a storage box. My parents installed it."

"Really?" Ambrose shot him a funny look, which I couldn't quite place. "It's empty now."

"Yeah, well, my mom was a compulsive cleaner. Probably hauled everything out before she passed away."

"A real trapdoor." Wonder tinged my voice. Now the store-bought china and plastic chandelier didn't seem quite so important. "How many houses have one of those?"

"Not many," Ambrose said.

"Well, it's getting late." Ashley made a big show out of checking his enormous Rolex. "No harm done. But it's time for me to close up the house."

"No problem," Ambrose said. "And we've got to go to the police station. Nice to meet you. Give us a shout if you need anything while you're in town."

"Sure. I'll do that."

Somehow I knew he wouldn't take Ambrose up on the offer. "Ambrose is right. We're just down the road. And one more thing." Even though this might not be the time nor the place, something else had been bugging me. "You might want to slow down when you drive around town. You don't want to get a speeding ticket."

Chapter 5

Ambrose and I left the mansion the same way we'd entered it: through a side door.

I finally turned to him when we reached the Audi. "All right, Ambrose Jackson. Spill it. You've been dying to tell me something. It's written all over your face."

"You know me too well." He opened my car door before walking around to the driver's side. "That guy is lying, Missy. There's no way his family put in that trapdoor."

I slid into the passenger's seat and waited for him to join me in the car. "Now how could you possibly know that?"

"Easy. The hinges were cast iron. That's why the door banged so loudly when I let it go."

I must've looked confused because he leaned toward me.

"Cast iron," he repeated. "Not stainless steel. Everyone started using stainless steel when it came out in the sixties. Those hinges are original to the house."

I studied his face, only inches from mine. His beautiful blue eyes looked serious now. "Wow. But what if Ashley didn't know any better? What if he just assumed his parents added it?"

"No, there's more to the story than that. He's hiding something." Ambrose straightened and turned on the car's engine.

"What do you know?" I tried to stifle a grin, without much luck. "Usually I'm the suspicious one, not you. What makes you say that?"

"That door was lined in lead." Though Ambrose somberly watched the road, his thoughts seemed a million miles away. "Which means they were worried about fire. Now, why would they worry about fire so much?"

"The house *is* made of wood. You know how paranoid people were about kitchen fires back then."

"But the kitchen's in the back of the house. No, there's more to it than that. And the house was built around the time of the Civil War. Maybe it had something to do with that."

"Cool! But why wouldn't Ashley admit it? Why would he lie to us?"

"Beats me."

Come to think of it, Ashley *did* seem desperate to escape the house once Ambrose discovered the trapdoor. Maybe that was why he made a big show of checking his watch. "By the way, did you see his Rolex?"

Ambrose guffawed. "Hard to miss. Pretty fancy for a guy his age."

"That's what I thought. A lot of things here don't add up. If he's got so much money, why's he in a panic to sell the house?"

"Good question."

"No matter what, I don't think he liked me very much."

"You're kidding, right?" Ambrose made a hard left. "Of course he liked you. He kept checking you out whenever you turned around. I caught him two or three times. Would've punched him if he did it again."

Now my grin blossomed into a full-blown smile. Not because of Ashley—I didn't care about him—but because of Ambrose's reaction. "Why, Ambrose Jackson. You sound jealous. That guy is young enough to be my kid brother. He also had a Yale key ring, so he's practically a Yankee."

"Really?" His tone was teasing. "But if you marry him, you could get that big old house in the bargain. He could be Rhett, and you could be Scarlett O'Hara."

I rolled my eyes. "Ashley was the one Scarlett wanted, not Rhett." Which was highly ironic, given the guy's name.

"Whatever. You could live in that big ol' house with your twelve kids and two nannies."

I reached over and pinched him, since I'd heard just about enough. Maybe that would put a stop to the teasing. "How about if you drive us to the police station and leave my love life alone?"

"Whatever you say, Scarlett."

Thankfully, he dropped the subject after that. Which left me free to think about other things, like the way my hair was beginning to stick to the back of my neck. The car felt stuffy, even with the luke-warm air blowing through the Audi's air-conditioning vents. That was one thing about living in a small Southern town: Everything was so close together cars never had a chance to really cool down in the summertime.

I cracked my window and fiddled with the knobs on the vents. At least the air became tolerable by the time we arrived at the police substation. We drove onto the sparse parking lot and Ambrose cut the ignition.

Our car joined two others. A new Ford Focus sat in a front space; probably owned by the radio dispatcher. The second, a dirty Louisiana state police squad car, sat two rows behind. Dried mud caked that car's undercarriage and its windshield looked like a strip of used fly-paper. It couldn't be, could it? I knew of only one police officer who'd treat his car like a sedan in a demolition derby.

"I do believe Lance LaPorte is here," I said.

"You mean the cop from Morningside?" Ambrose sounded skep-tical.

That was many months ago, when I'd landed smack-dab in the middle of another crime scene, this time at Morningside. After I fin-gered the person responsible for the bride's death, the killer tried to get me too, until Lance arrived and put a stop to that nonsense.

"The very same."

Lance's boss had promoted him to the criminal-investigations division around the same time, if I recalled correctly, and now St. James Parish must've called him back to investigate Mellette's murder.

"He'd definitely drive that car."

We made our way to the substation, passing under a sign that read *Troop C of the Louisiana State Police.* As soon as we ducked into the lobby, the sweat on my collar began to dry.

Along with being over–air-conditioned, the room we entered was entirely beige, as if a cleaning crew had tried to bleach the color away. A row of tan filing cabinets ran along an off-white wall, be-hind which four battered beige desks angled to face each other.

Maybe that was why Lance stood out in his navy-blue police uni-form. He stood behind a low counter that separated visitors from em-ployees, and I spotted him right away.

"I knew it!" I said.

Lance glanced up. He'd been reading from a manila file folder, which he snapped shut. "Why, Missy DuBois. Butter my butt and call me a biscuit. What're you doing here?"

"I could ask you the same thing."

When he grinned, the gap-toothed kid who sat next to me in Sunday school reappeared. The same one who ogled naked pictures of Adam and Eve in the Bible instead of memorizing verses, like we were supposed to do. I surely hoped he'd matured since then, since he now wore a shiny badge *and* a sinister-looking sidearm.

"Just doing my job."

"What, they only call you in when there's a murder at a fancy house?" I asked.

"Ain't that the truth. Let me guess . . . you had something to do with this one too?"

I waggled my finger at him. "Don't mock me, Lance. It's not my fault people around me keep turning up dead. You remember Ambrose, don't you?"

"Of course. Hi, Bo."

I waited for the men to exchange nods. "Ambrose and I were the ones who found the body this morning at Sweetwater."

He dropped the file folder to the counter, where a foil seal on its cover glimmered prettily under the fluorescent lights. The seal of the St. James Parish coroner's office was impossible to miss, even upside down.

"Speaking of Sweetwater," Ambrose said. "We came to see the officer who was at the house this morning."

Lance shook his head. "Sorry. He already went home. You should tell me about it, though."

"Okay," I said. "But promise you won't think we're crazy."

"No guarantees. You and I go too far back for that, Missy."

"Very funny." I should've reached across the counter and pinched him, but this didn't seem like the time, nor the place. "Anyway, Ambrose found the strangest thing out by the body this morning. A cross. And there was blood on it too."

Lance cocked his head. "I saw the pictures. The responding officer took 'em before he bagged and tagged it. Looked like a plain wood cross."

I lowered my voice. "That's the thing." The dispatcher—no doubt the owner of the new Ford Focus outside—was on the other side of the room, but it was better to be safe than sorry. "You know there's a caretaker at Sweetwater. A gal by the name of Ruby. I went to her place today." My voice fell even further. "It was chock-full of crosses. You should've seen it."

Lance didn't seem surprised by my news. "Yeah, we all know Ruby. We've been out to her place a coupla times. All domestic incidents."

My mind reeled back to Ruby's mobile home, where a lanky sixteen-year-old with dirty-blond hair had emerged from the shadows. "Was her grandson involved in those?"

"That's confidential. Let's just say that family has a mess of problems."

"But what about the crosses? Do you think the one by the body could've belonged to her?"

"Hard to know. Especially 'til the prints come back. We're waiting on those, and the coroner's report."

Not that I wanted to snoop—well, maybe a little—but the shiny logo on the folder in front of me glimmered like pond water. I pointed at it. "Isn't that the coroner's report?"

"No. It's too soon for anything official," he said. "That's just a list of things the medical examiner will look for. Things like sexual assault, drug use, that kind of thing. Evidence that might point to someone."

Several images immediately began to float through my mind. Memories of people I'd spoken with, like Ruby, the caretaker and Hollis, her grandson. With Beatrice, even.

"What about poisons?" I asked. "Someone said it looked like she could've been poisoned with acid because of her skin tone."

"It's hard to tell. We won't get the tox report back for several weeks, and that's the only way to know for sure."

I couldn't resist a minute longer, so I reached for the folder. "I can tell you right now the victim didn't look like she'd been sexually assaulted."

"Whoa." Lance reached for my wrist. "Right now, everything is conjecture."

It was happening all over again. Just like the episode at Morningside, when Lance wouldn't give me a lick of information until he'd thought I'd earned it. He wanted to make me work for it, apparently. "Okay, I get it. But remember what I said about Ruby."

"I won't count her out. But we don't have a primary suspect at this point."

"By the way, the victim wasn't on drugs." I eased my wrist away from his hand. "She looked fine to me when I saw her this morning."

"Maybe she put on a good act."

I shook my head. "You don't get it. We were in the same sorority and everything. She was an overachiever even back then. And she looked as healthy as a horse this morning."

"Let's see what the preliminary report says, okay? Right now, you and Ambrose should go home and try to decompress. You know . . . do relaxation exercises or something."

"Bless your heart," I said. "You're quoting from one of those police manuals. But I get it. Just let us know if you need help."

"Agreed," Ambrose said. "We got a real eyeful this morning."

"I'll do that." Lance finally seemed like his old self again. "And we need to catch up, Missy. Did you hear Mama opened her second restaurant right here in Bleu Bayou? Whoo-ee . . . that woman is on fire."

"I heard about that. Good for her. We can go there, or wherever else you want. You choose. I'm not picky."

I purposefully avoided Ambrose's gaze just then, since I knew he'd be rolling his eyes. Instead, I threw Lance a smile and backed away from the folder.

Chapter 6

The late-afternoon sun felt wonderful on my shoulders after the chill of the police station. I followed Ambrose to the Audi, where he opened my door before settling into the driver's seat.

"That was interesting," I said.

"Which part?"

Where to begin? "For one thing, the stuff the medical examiner will look for. I hadn't even thought of assault. But I'm telling you, Mellette didn't look like she'd been assaulted."

"Maybe the person assaulted her somewhere else and then brought her body back to the cottage."

I thought it over as Ambrose started the Audi and we pulled away from the lot.

"But there weren't any drag marks on the floor," I finally said. "We would've noticed that with the dust. And her clothes looked fine to me. They hadn't been messed up. Kinda looked like she was sleeping."

"Except for her legs." Ambrose spoke slowly. "They were all crumpled up. And her head was at a weird angle."

"That's right. I forgot you had to stay with her until the police came. Sorry about that. But I *do* know Lance is wrong about drugs. Can't imagine any sorority sister overdosing."

"But you haven't seen her in—what's it been—ten years? Maybe something happened to her after college."

"Don't you think I would've noticed if something was wrong this morning? She was right as rain. No, I won't even consider it."

Ambrose pulled into the next lane. "Lance *did* say he wants to meet up with you tomorrow. Maybe he'll speak his mind when he's away from the police station. Especially if you load him up with a big plate of food. Speaking of which, you look pale. When's the last time you had anything to eat?"

Sweet of him to notice. "I don't remember. This morning? And you're right. I'm so hungry I could eat the backside of a skunk."

"Me too," he said. "Where do you want to go?"

Good question. Although I'd promised myself I wouldn't be so bossy in the future, Lance had reminded me of something I'd long forgotten.

Years ago and miles away, when Lance and I were just kids, we whiled away the summer days playing slapjack at his house. Then we headed to his kitchen, since his mom made the best fried chicken on the block. Not to mention the world's lightest butter biscuits, which twisted apart like Oreos.

But it was the smell I remembered most. Warm butter and cooking oil, thick enough to keep us kids inside on even the most glorious summer day. Since that time, Miss Odilia had opened two restaurants, like Lance said, with one of them being down the road from us. I'd read a review in the *Bleu Bayou Impartial Reporter*, but had forgotten all about it with the hullaballoo at Sweetwater.

Even before the review, I'd seen workers buzzing around a 1930s gingerbread house downtown. Chunks of shag carpeting and wallpapered Sheetrock had been piled up outside the front door during the transformation. At one point a massive range hood moved in and a dingy bathtub moved out. The last time I drove by, there was a sign that announced the grand opening of Miss Odilia's Southern Eatery.

"Lance said something about his mom's new restaurant," I said. "She makes the best Southern fried chicken of anyone."

"But didn't he want to take you there tomorrow?"

"Sure, but it couldn't hurt to preview it. I don't mind going two times in a row."

"Okay, then. Where is it?"

"Not too far off."

It wasn't hard to find once we'd passed our shops. I pointed out two left turns and one right and, within a few minutes, we reached the parking lot.

Compared to the fancier places in town, Miss Odilia's Southern Eatery was nothing special on the outside. The red brick walls had gone pink with age, and the same bricks covered a chimney. Over the door hung a kelly-green awning and purple window boxes bloomed with freshly planted flowers.

But simple or not, a line of cars zigged and zagged through the parking lot. We weren't the only ones curious about the new restaurant. By the time we joined the lineup and found a parking space, my stomach gurgled like a teapot brought to a boil.

I practically raced to the front door, notwithstanding my pledge to be less feisty in the future. An old man held the door open for me, apparently the last person in a line that snaked all the way to a hostess stand.

Ambrose frowned. "Think Lance's mother can help us out here?"

"I don't know. She might not even be here. She's got the other restaurant too."

Glumly, I eyed the crowd. Most of the people around us were grouped in families, like the senior who'd helped me with the door. He was surrounded by a group of teenagers, who I guessed to be his grandchildren. A few steps ahead a young mother held a drooling infant propped over her shoulder.

"You stay here," Ambrose said. "I'll go to the front and see what the wait's like."

"Yes, sir." Normally I would've saluted too, but this didn't seem like the time, nor the place. Instead, I dug in my heels and surveyed the line again.

Turned out the man standing in front of me was a Navy veteran, according to an emblem on his bomber jacket. His grandkids were all a foot taller, and they crouched forward whenever the old man spoke. Meanwhile, the baby up ahead gummed a Saltine cracker until it became a messy paste.

I couldn't see anyone else in line. Only when the baby pitched forward in her mother's arms did I spy the next customer, who wore a dress shirt covered with gold and purple fleurs-de-lis. It looked like something LSU's mascot might cough up after licking its fur. Where had I seen that hideous pattern before? And then I remembered. The break room, on a calendar Beatrice had tacked to the wall. The one with her uncle, Hank Dupre.

It couldn't be. Could it?

Stretching on my tiptoes, I peered around the senior in the bomber jacket. It was Hank Dupre all right, and he stood beside a guy with the strangest haircut: bushy on top and shaved clean at the sides. It was Ashley Cox. But didn't Ashley say he didn't know anyone in town?

"Hey, I'm back." Ambrose returned, looking a little winded.

"Hallelujah. Now go back up there and talk to the hostess or something. I need a minute to check out a hunch."

"Why would I do that? It's a madhouse up there."

"Because." I pulled him close. "Look up ahead, just past the baby. That godawful shirt in purple and gold. It's Hank Dupre, Beatrice's uncle. He's the one who loaned us the boat today."

"What do you know." Ambrose chuckled. "That's quite a shirt. We could go say hello, but *after* we eat."

"There's more." I yanked him closer. "Look again. Do you see who he's talking to? It's Ashley Cox, from the house. The guy who told us he didn't know anyone here."

"Guess he knows at least one person."

"But don't you think that's strange?" I asked. "And it's Beatrice's uncle, of all people."

Ambrose blew out a puff of air. "Maybe they have a family connection. And didn't you say the uncle's a real estate agent? Could be he just wants the listing for Ashley's house."

"Maybe. But it's awfully soon after Mellette's death for someone to come sniffing around for one of her listings." Though, to be honest, her uncle *had* given me his business card when I mentioned my interest in Sweetwater. Maybe Ambrose was right. Maybe the meeting was purely business, after all.

"Excuse me." A figure rushed past, heading into the restaurant, shoving me into Ambrose's side.

"Lorda mercy!" I said.

The culprit, a waiter in a black apron and a pressed white shirt, suddenly stopped. "I'm sorry, but I'm late."

In addition to the black-and-white getup, streaks of silver shot through the guy's dark hair.

Why, I'd know that salt-and-pepper combination anywhere. "Charles?"

His eyes widened. "Is that you, Miss DuBois?"

He always did have nice manners. He looked more haggard since the last time we'd met, no doubt because he took classes at LSU and worked too.

"I told you to call me Missy. And I haven't seen you since Morningside!"

That was a while ago, when I'd arrived at Morningside for the ill-fated wedding. As luck would have it, I sat at one of Charles's tables in the dining room on my very first night there. Too bad Herbert Solomon had bought the mansion and fired everyone, including Charles.

"I thought you were gonna start a waitstaff service with some of the other waiters who used to work at Morningside," I said.

"We did." He shrugged listlessly. He'd definitely aged since our last meeting. "We do catering on the side. I told Miss Odilia I'd work here too. What about you?"

At this point, the drooling baby up ahead decided to howl, so I raised my voice to compensate. "I've been busy. Really, really busy."

"Look, it's too crowded," Charles said. "Come with me."

He quickly disappeared, leaving me no choice but to signal Ambrose. "C'mon, Bo. You remember Charles, don't you?"

I dashed behind Charles as he retreated through the front door and down the walk. He moved so fast—all nervous energy—my side ached by the time we reached the rear of the house. Once there, we faced a door marked *employees only*, which Charles strong-armed until it opened.

The kitchen was bright and as hot as a gas burner. A few servers walked through clouds of steam, carrying dinner plates loaded with fried chicken and what looked like spoonfuls of jelly.

"They've *got* to fix the employees' door," Charles said. "That's why I parked on the street and went through the front door."

Then he took off again, which meant Ambrose and I could either keep up with him or be left behind. We chose to hustle and stayed on his heels all the way through the kitchen. Finally, we passed through a swinging door that propelled us into the dining room.

Compared to the kitchen, this room was soft and homey and quiet, with chintz curtains and polished wood tables and captain's chairs with rounded arms.

Diners filled the room. Only one table sat empty, and that was stuck in an awkward alcove across the way. There was barely enough headroom for someone to sit upright, but that's where Charles pointed. "You can sit there. I have to clock in."

"No, we couldn't." I reached out to stop him, and not just because of the table's placement. "There are too many people waiting in line. It's not a great spot, but you should at least offer it to one of them first. Especially that poor mama with the fussy baby."

"But we haven't been using it. We call it 'no-man's-land.' If you don't use it, no one will."

I studied his eyes, which looked sincere enough. "Promise? Okay, then. But try to get that family a table too."

"Okay. Back in two seconds."

Ambrose and I headed for no-man's-land, while Charles went to clock in and speak to the hostess.

I ducked under the crossbeam and settled into the captain's chair. The table immediately wobbled. "Well, it *is* a table."

"Technically, yes." Ambrose braced his palms on the surface to steady it. "Good thing we didn't come here for the ambience."

"It's only been open a few days. Everyone knows all new restaurants have kinks. I'll tell Mrs. LaPorte she should turn this spot into a waiter's station or something."

"It'd be perfect for the busboys."

"At least we didn't have to confront Ashley right away. I'm still trying to figure out what he's doing here with Beatrice's uncle, of all people."

"Could be nothing." Ambrose's gaze swept over the bare table. "Looks like we don't have any menus. I'll have to take your word for it on what to order."

"Go with the fried chicken. You can't go wrong with that. She used to make it for Lance and me back when we were just little kids. Everybody on our whole block went crazy for it. That and her butter biscuits."

By the time we had settled on that, Charles was back. His hair looked wild from all of the coming and going, and a lock of it stood straight up. My assistant, Beatrice, had always commented on his crazy hair when the two were dating.

"Tonight's special is fried catfish with lemon cream," he said.

I smoothed some of my hair down, hoping he'd take the hint.

"Missy here has been telling me all about the fried chicken," Ambrose said.

"Can't go wrong with that."

Unfortunately, Charles didn't catch the clue I was trying to throw him, and I lowered my hand. "By the way, have you talked to Beatrice recently? I know you two went on a couple of dates, but I haven't heard anything since."

He shrugged, the shock of hair bobbing along. "I don't know what her problem is. We were doing fine until she freaked out. Guess she wanted to be more serious than I did."

"Hmmm." *Now that didn't sound right.* Beatrice wasn't serious about much of anything, except for fashion, and then she was downright passionate. She did say Charles was too unpredictable, or something like that, but she wouldn't gossip behind his back. "You don't say. That's too bad. I always thought you two would make a good couple."

"Missy." Ambrose shot me a look that warned me not to overstep my bounds.

"What?" I said. "Can't a girl ask an innocent question?"

"It's okay," Charles said. "We kind of left it open. So, what about the fried chicken?"

"Perfect," Ambrose said. "And some butter biscuits. Missy has been pining for those since we got here."

"Not to switch subjects," I said, although I had every intention of doing just that, "but you wouldn't believe what happened to us today. Ambrose and I went to the old Sweetwater mansion this morning."

"Whoa." Charles's eyes darkened. "That place is messed up."

"You must have heard about the murder. We were the ones who found the victim in the shed."

"You know what they say about that place, right? It's haunted."

"C'mon. It's probably just rumors. You know how stuff like that gets around." For some reason, I felt protective of the old mansion, as if I needed to guard it against naysayers. That hadn't changed since the moment I'd stepped onto its lush grounds.

"Uh-huh." Charles didn't look convinced. "I'm not sure that going over there is such a good idea. You two should probably stay away."

"Why, Charles." I said. "Can't imagine why you'd talk ugly about one of the prettiest houses I've ever seen."

"Yeah, but you haven't lived very long in this town. I have. Some weird stuff goes on down there. Better for you to keep your distance."

Ambrose straightened next to me. "That's right . . . you grew up here. What do folks say?"

"Just take my word for it," Charles said.

"Okay, okay." I threw up my hands. "No need to get all worked up."

"I'm serious. You two shouldn't mess with that place. You don't know what you're getting yourself into."

His scolding caused my cheeks to heat. "Fine. We'll order and try to forget all about Sweetwater for a while. By the way, we don't have any silverware. Could you please bring some?"

"Sure thing." He shot Ambrose a final look. "Maybe you can talk some sense into her."

"I'll try." Ambrose sounded resigned, as if he knew he was in for an uphill battle. He waited for Charles to disappear before he spoke again. "Boy, does he think that house is bad news."

"I know. But Mellette would've warned me if something was wrong with it. She called all that voodoo stuff 'hooey.'"

"Think about it." Now even Ambrose sounded spooked. "She also was trying to sell the place. Would you tell a client about something like that?"

Why does everyone insist on bad-mouthing Sweetwater? "I would. And she was my sorority sister." Enough was enough, already. "I don't know why people are so set against that house. Can we drop the subject now?"

Finally, his jaw relaxed. "You're right. And the good news is Mrs. LaPorte's restaurant looks like it's a hit. The food here must be great."

"It is." Only then did I notice something else was missing from our table. Something crucial, after the day we'd had. "We don't have wineglasses, either."

"I can fix that." Ambrose rose, ducking his head to avoid hitting the crossbeams. "There's a bar out front, behind that long line we were in. What would you like?"

"White wine, please. I think we've both earned it after the day we've had."

He flashed a grin. "You got it. And don't look so worried. I'll be right back."

The minute he left, I settled back. My gaze flickered to the dining room, or at least the parts of it I could see. Most everyone was grouped in threes and fours. A hostess struggled to wedge a high chair under one of the tables, which meant Charles must have wrangled a spot for the mother and her baby after all.

After a minute or so, someone stepped in front of me and blocked my view.

"Why, Missy DuBois!" Odilia LaPorte, her snowy hair wound in a chignon tonight, towered over me. "Whatever are you doing here?"

The mother who fed me fried chicken on those summer days so many years ago. She ducked the crossbeams too, and took Ambrose's seat. "What a terrible spot for a table! I'll have to tell my staff. C'mon, let's get you a proper seat."

"No, no. It's fine," I lied. "I'm comfortable enough. How are you?"

"Good. I'm doing good."

She looked good. A sprinkle of flour dusted her apron, and her moon face glowed under the old-fashioned Tiffany lamps. "So, who're you here with?"

"Ambrose Jackson. You remember him, don't you? He's the one who came with me to Morningside Plantation last May."

She tittered. "Do I ever. How is that fine-lookin' man doing?"

Not only did I meet up with Charles on that trip, but I was able to reunite with Odilia as well. We ate dinner one night, and she confided she'd been working quietly behind the scenes for several years to get two restaurants up and running. She'd been planning it all with an architect, without telling a soul.

"It's not what you think," I said. "Ambrose and I are friends. Good friends."

She chuckled again. "Um-hum. I'll bet you are. When will one of you make a move, like I told you? Don't be so old-fashioned. Nowadays a lot of girls make the first move."

"I don't know what you're talking about." My words might have been more believable if a giant grin hadn't appeared on my face.

She jabbed a finger at me. "Sooner or later one of you is going to have to gin up and say something. *Gah-lee*. And let me tell you, it's about time you two came to this restaurant. We've been open three whole days already, and this is the first time I've seen you."

I winced. She was right. "Sorry about that. Things have been kinda crazy. I'm proud of you, though. We had to circle the parking lot three times to find a space."

She waved away the compliment, but only halfheartedly. "You always were my favorite child back in the neighborhood. Speaking of which . . . have you seen my Lance lately? You and he made a fine team back then."

"I saw him this afternoon. He's helping the police here with a murder investigation. Only this one happened at Sweetwater mansion. Did he tell you about that?"

"He did indeed." The smile slipped from her face. "What's the world coming to? I told that boy he needs to be more careful out there. You never know how these things will turn out."

"I suppose. The really strange thing is I knew the gal. We were sorority sisters at Vanderbilt. Can't imagine why someone would kill her."

"Me, either." She leaned in a tad. "But it was only a matter of time before something bad happened at that house. You know what they say about it, right? A voodoo queen uses it for some kind of ceremony. Every month is what I've heard tell."

Here we go again. "You don't say."

"Um-mmm." Her eyes looked troubled. "This time's different, though. Mother Belle—she's the voodoo queen—performs all kinda rituals there, but not the killing kind. No, this time's different, all right."

"Now, Miss Odilia. People keep bad-mouthing that plantation house to me. But how do you know it's true?"

"True?" She looked surprised, as if the answer should've been obvious. "Why, Charles told me. He's friends with all those folks."

My mouth fell open. Charles? The one who tried to convince Ambrose and me to stay away from the mansion? How could he know those people?

Before I could respond, a noise sounded behind Odilia. It was Ambrose, bearing a bottle of Chardonnay and two wineglasses.

"Why, hello there." He reached over Odilia's head to place the glasses on the table.

Odilia craned her neck. "Look at you, Ambrose Jackson. As handsome as ever. Hmmm, mmm."

"How much do I owe you for saying that?" He winked as he sat on the last empty chair.

"I'll take a good restaurant review for starters. But it looks like y'all are about to have your dinner, so I won't interrupt. Only came in tonight to work with the chef since that poor boy can't tell the difference between chutney and plain ol' jelly."

I reached for her hand. "Don't go. We were talking about Charles."

"Let's save that for another time." Gently, she loosened my hand and lumbered to her feet. "A lot of it's hearsay, anyway. And Lord knows what's been going on in my kitchen since I've been out here yapping. Excuse me."

She stepped around Ambrose and began to sashay through the dining room, every once in a while leaning over to speak with a patron.

"She seems nice," Ambrose said, once she'd disappeared. "Busy, but nice."

"You don't know the half of it."

He motioned to the wine bottle. "First things first. You look pale. Maybe a drink will help. It's not the best vintage, but it'll do."

"I just heard something about Charles." Could Odilia be right? Maybe I didn't hear her correctly. "It's probably nothing. Let's forget about Sweetwater for one night. It's all we've been talking about and my head hurts."

"Deal." Ambrose poured Chardonnay into a glass for me. "By the way, my first choice would've been a nice cabernet. That's what I order on special occasions."

"Don't worry. This is fine." Hallelujah, my day was finally turning around, even though I had to wait fifteen hours for it to happen.

Chapter 7

An hour later, I pushed aside my empty plate with a grunt. "I'm gonna burst. This very second. Don't laugh."

"No one ever spontaneously combusted in a restaurant." Ambrose didn't even try to suppress a chuckle. "But I promise I'll pick up the pieces if you do."

"Lean over here so I can pinch you."

He finally stopped mocking me long enough to point to a pair of empty wine bottles on the table. "Looks like we killed 'em. I must say, you have an impressive appetite for a woman your size."

"It's the first time I've eaten since breakfast. I told you . . . she makes the best fried chicken around."

Ambrose turned to appraise the restaurant behind him. Most of the diners were long gone, and he slowly turned around again. "You know, we probably shouldn't spend the night here. The waiters will talk. Let's get you in the car."

He began to rise but immediately smacked his head against the crossbeam. "Damn! Forgot that was there."

"Are you sure you're okay to drive?" I asked. "You might want to give me the car keys."

"No, no. I'm fine. I've just got a rude headache now." He paused before trying again, and this time he offered me his hand.

I placed my palm in his and shakily rose to my feet. For some reason the ceiling tilted crazily. "Well, this is going to be interesting."

"You're doing great." He gently led me away from the table and into the restaurant. Soon we wobbled past an older couple who had taken the place of the young family; the ground beneath their chairs was dusted with bread crumbs, smashed Cheerios, and juice stains. A middle-aged couple sat not too far away. I resisted the urge to steady my hand on their table as I walked by.

After a minute, Ambrose veered right, to a part of the dining room I hadn't seen before. Here, pretty mullioned windows lined the wall and each had a flower box under it. Even in my stupor, I noticed Odilia had chosen the same flowers—foxglove, caladium, and calla lilies—that she used outside. By the very last flower box sat two men with suit coats slung over their chairs. A ridiculous pattern splashed across the older man's back.

"Gol-darn it."

"Huh?" Ambrose paused next to me. "What's up?"

"That's Hank Dupre. With Ashley Cox." Apparently they'd finished their meal, because soiled napkins covered their dinner plates.

Ambrose tried to pull me forward, but my feet were stuck to the carpet. "C'mon, Missy." His tug grew more insistent. "Let's go."

"Don't you see them?"

He stopped tugging. "Yeah, I do."

Both of us were whispering, the words thick and sluggish.

"What are they doing here?"

"I don't know." Ambrose's eyes darted to the front door. "Okay. Let's get out of here. We can talk about it in the car."

We tottered away from the men and swerved toward the front door. Once we emerged outside, I realized Ambrose had taken my hand. I tried to focus on the feel of his palm, the sound of the cicadas nearby, and the lingering smells of oil and car exhaust. Anything but the smarmy grins on the two men's faces.

By the time we found his car and drove away from the restaurant, my head had begun to clear.

Seeing the two men had sobered me up like a splash of ice water. "Why would Ashley Cox meet with Hank Dupre?"

"I told you, I don't know. Maybe it has something to do with real estate. Could be he's giving Dupre the listing."

"It's a little soon, don't you think?"

Ambrose glanced at the rearview mirror. "Got any better ideas?"

I began to chew my lower lip, which still tasted sweet from the Chardonnay. "The whole thing seems sketchy."

Ambrose glanced at me from the corner of his eye. "Even if it *is* sketchy, there's nothing we can do about it. Let's just make it home in one piece tonight."

He was right, of course. The day had been overly long and utterly exhausting, without my dramatics. We fell silent as the car passed the Factory, the building's roofline pitched and dark against the midnight sky. A few miles later, Dippin' Donuts appeared, also mired in shadows. Amazing to think Grady, the owner, would strike the lights in only a few hours. A mile or so down lay Sweetwater, and then our cozy rent house with its cotton-candy walls and listing garden gate.

Ambrose suddenly leaned forward. "What the hell?"

Sweetwater appeared, all right, the opening between the live oaks like the gaping mouth of a cave. But behind the row of tress and the darkened mansion rose an even odder sight: A pulsing, effervescent light.

The light roiled.

"Should we stop the car?" My voice came out high and tight.

"No, I'm driving closer." Ambrose inched the car forward and then turned off the road and parked. "I'll be damned."

"What do you suppose it is?" The glow splashed shadows onto the trees like ink being thrown against parchment.

Instead of answering, Ambrose reached for the handle of his car door. "Hell if I know. I'll check it out while you wait here."

"No, you don't. You're not leaving me here. I'm going with you." Quickly, I grabbed for my door handle too.

Out shot his arm. "No way, Missy."

Damn him and his quick reflexes! "Let me go, Ambrose."

"You stay put. I mean it. I'll be back in a few minutes. Don't move."

I collapsed into the seat, deflated. "Fine. But if you take too long, I'm coming to get you."

"Deal." He finally removed his hand and then switched off the headlights. Everything disappeared but the light show up ahead.

His car door creaked open as he folded out, and then the crunch of his shoes on the pea gravel sounded. He must have forgotten something, though, because he returned a few seconds later.

"What now?" I asked.

"I'm not kidding. Don't follow me." With that, he slammed the door shut.

Fine by me. I began to mull my options. It seemed I could either stay in the car and wait patiently for his return or make myself useful and join him. Who was I kidding? With a deep breath, I slid out of the car. Thank goodness the ground didn't tilt this time, like it had at the restaurant.

Since Ambrose had disappeared straight ahead, I chose to zigzag across the front lawn, moving from oak to oak. As I approached the mansion, the leaves began to pulse to a faint beat; one that was hollow but insistent. Afterward came the reedy notes of a flute, almost as high as a bird's call.

My heart quickened. By pinballing from one gnarled oak to the next, I soon arrived at the side of the house and peered around the corner. A small crowd had gathered around a fire pit about the size of a child's wading pool. Flames shot up from the pit's center.

The group linked arms around the fire, and everyone stared at the person who seemed to be in charge. She was a tall, African-American woman, who towered over them on a ladder propped against the pit. She wore a batik headdress, a speckled ivory scarf, and a wraparound skirt. When she opened her mouth, the reedy soprano I'd heard earlier poured out. Higher and higher she sang, the words hopscotching over one another:

> *I—the Voodoo Queen,*
> *With my lovely head kerchief*
> *Am not afraid of tomcat shrieks,*
> *For I drink serpent venom!*

Every once in a while, the woman grasped her scarf and twisted it, as if it were a wet dish towel in need of wringing.

"What are you doing here?"

I flinched and turned.

Ambrose stood right beside me, as unexpected as a lightning strike.

"Don't do that! You scared me half to death!"

"Me? You're not supposed to be here."

"Shhh." The last thing we needed was to be spotted by the crowd. "Do you want them to hear us?"

"What I want *you* to do is go back to the car."

I pointed at the singer. "But what's she doing?" Maybe if I distracted him, Ambrose would let me stay.

"Beats me." He reached for something in his pocket. "But I have a feeling we can find someone who knows." Out came his cell, which he turned to *record* by pushing a button on the screen.

"Brilliant," I said.

Now the scarf around the singer's neck began to writhe, as if it was folding inward to escape the heat. The woman held one end between her thumb and index finger, while the other end flailed.

"My god," Ambrose said. "She's wearing a snake."

"She can't be."

"I swear that's a buttermilk racer."

Blithely, the singer plucked the racer from around her neck and began to swing it over the flame. All the while she sang:

> *Ena! Ena!*
> *Akout, Akout an deye*
> *Jocomo fi nou wa na né*
> *Jockomo fi na né*

"*Akou!*" the crowd responded.

As Ambrose's cell captured the singing, I studied the faces in the firelight. Most belonged to middle-aged women dressed in batik cloth. Whorls of color and splashes of dye appeared on knotted head scarves, loose dresses, and flowing skirts swept to one side. A few of the women cradled drowsy babies on their shoulders. No one spoke, except for a shouted response or two.

Behind the scene, almost hidden by an enormous oak, stood a lone figure. The wan teenager had dirty-blond hair and a slight build, and he wore the same sleeveless T-shirt and running shorts I'd seen before. At a derelict mobile home, wasn't it?

Hollis Oubre, Ruby's grandson, stared at the fire pit, along with the rest of the crowd.

When the singer arced the snake higher and higher, prepared to dash it into the fire, I lurched forward.

"Don't. Not yet." Ambrose had clamped his hand on my shoulder.

The poor animal thrashed. At the last second, the singer changed her mind and flung it into a clearing at the edge of the property, where it landed with a thud and then barrel-rolled away.

No one moved. The only sound was the snap and pop of burning wood. Just when I thought the silence would go on forever, that we'd all stare at the fire until nothing was left but smoke and embers, a noise hummed next to me. A different noise, which began softly and quickly crescendoed. It was the opening notes of a trumpet melody. And it sounded suspiciously like the fight song for Auburn University.

"Ambrose!"

He'd downloaded that song as a ringtone only a week ago.

Quickly, he slapped at the phone and the music died. But it was too late. The crowd turned in unison to stare at us. Everyone looked amazed, as if we'd been the ones who were conjured by fire and might disappear in a puff of smoke.

Ambrose grabbed my hand. "Let's go."

There was no time to think, no time to do anything but follow him as he pulled me away from the crowd.

Thankfully, no one came after us. Then again, my heart beat so loudly in my chest that all other noise fell away. We ran through the front yard and barreled through the live oaks lining the walk. I stumbled on an exposed root and nearly fell but, thankfully, Ambrose steadied me.

When we arrived at the Audi, he threw open my car door. "Hop in!"

I jumped onto the seat and he slammed the door. Then he ran over to his side, jumped into the driver's seat and engaged the ignition, before we finally roared away.

I tumbled against the seat cushion. Could it be that only a few minutes earlier we'd arrived at Sweetwater on little cat feet, as that famous poet would say? We'd even doused the headlights for good measure.

Now we careened down the driveway, the scenery jerking by my window. Instead of watching the trees, though, I stared through the windshield. The image of a writhing snake danced before my eyes, and then an awestruck crowd and a wan teenager who skulked in the background. What was Hollis Oubre doing there?

More images came to mind. Flames that splashed white against the trees. The shock on Ambrose's face when his cell phone sounded. And the way we'd crashed through the woods afterward.

A giggle suddenly tickled the back of my throat. I gulped, trying to squelch it, but it refused to back down. After a minute, I gave in and burst out laughing.

Ambrose eyed me as if I was insane. Then, gradually, his shoulders trembled and a laugh worked its way out.

"Ambrose!" I couldn't watch him and hope to catch my breath, so I twisted in my seat and faced the door. Ropey vines rolled past the window, the shadowy kudzu still devouring everything in its path. "Stop it! I can't breathe."

"What?" He spoke between peals of laughter. "*It's. Not. My. Fault.*"

All the while we continued to drive, darkness blotting out the familiar sights.

"By the way," I finally said. "Who would be calling you at one in the morning?"

"Hell if I know." He took a deep breath. "Probably a crazy bride. Wants to change her hemline or something."

"You know they coulda roasted us back there. Forget the snake— we were next!"

That brought on more laughter. Good thing he was an excellent driver and he maneuvered the steering wheel with one hand while he held his side with the other.

"You're hopeless." Finally, I lowered my feet back to the floorboards. "What are we gonna do with you?"

"Me? I remember telling you to stay in the car, where you'd be safe. No one asked you to come out like that."

"I'm glad I did. I wouldn't have missed that for the world. A real voodoo ceremony. It was the queen Odilia told me about . . . Mother Belle. I'm sure of it."

"Queen?"

I nodded, although he wasn't watching me. "Odilia said there's a voodoo queen around here who does something called black magick."

"She looked possessed. And that chant—"

"Thank goodness you got it on your phone. I'll play it for Ruby in the morning." My thoughts returned to the caretaker and her derelict mobile home by the dock. The one with a mishmash of crosses and a sallow teenager in the kitchen. The memories quickly sobered me up.

"I forgot to tell you," I said. "I recognized someone back there."

"Who?"

"The kid in shorts. Way in the back. It was Ruby's grandson, Hollis. He lives with her."

"Guess he also goes to voodoo ceremonies."

"That's the thing. It's awful late for him to be out on a school night."

Ambrose shrugged. "Maybe he's homeschooled."

"That's what he said. But I didn't see any textbooks or papers or even a computer at his house."

"Interesting." Ambrose reached into the pocket of his jeans, and then he pulled out the cell and tossed it to me. "Maybe his grandmother can make some sense of this tomorrow."

I caught the phone warily, as if it might burn my fingers. Although I'd offered to hunt down Ruby and play the recording for her, part of me wished I'd never made that promise. I quickly glanced at the call log on his phone. "By the way, your call back there came from the 228 area code."

"Mississippi? I've got a bride from Gulfport right now. Crazy as hell. No doubt it was her."

"Okay, Ambrose." I slowly lowered the phone. "I'll go back to Ruby's place. But now that I've seen an actual voodoo queen, I've got a bad feeling about this."

Chapter 8

I awoke the next morning to a soft knock on my bedroom door. Daylight slanted through the window and pooled beside me on the bed. Groaning, I rolled over and closed my eyes again.

"You awake?"

It was Ambrose, of course, speaking to me from the other side of the door. Why did I have to live with such an early riser?

"No. Go away." Grudgingly, I popped one eye open and squinted at the clock on my nightstand. "It's only been five hours. Let me sleep." A second later, guilt kicked in. "All right. Come on in if you have to."

The door swept open and he entered the room with a heavy sterling tray. He'd loaded the antique tray, which we normally reserved for guests, with a stack of blueberry pancakes and a giant coffee mug.

"Here you go, sleeping beauty." He gently placed the bounty on the mattress beside me.

I uncurled my legs and sat up. *First things first.* Steam rose from the coffee mug as I brought it to my lips. After two sips, I found my voice. "You're too good to me, Bo."

"Probably. But we had a rough time last night." He had eased himself onto a corner of the mattress, careful not to jiggle the tray.

"Okay . . . I give up," I said. "Why are we awake so early?"

"Fair question. Remember that phone call last night?"

"How could I forget?"

He passed me a fork from the tray. "I was right. It was the bride from Gulfport."

"At one in the morning?" I took the fork and stabbed the top pancake. Sometimes Bo's clients had no respect for his time. Even though he didn't seem to care, *I* did. He was much too talented for that. "I hope you told her off."

"Really?" He arched an eyebrow. "That's your secret for keeping customers? Actually, I called her back from the kitchen and made an appointment with her for this morning. Might as well get it over with."

"This morning? But Bo . . ." There went my plan to spend a few hours with him as I slowly recovered from the craziness of the night before.

"I know . . . I don't like it either. But she's panicked. And I took a call for you right afterward."

"Me?" I bit into the warm pancake, the blueberry juice flavoring it perfectly.

"It was Lance LaPorte. He's at the police station and he wants to talk to you."

It seemed like days—not just hours—since I'd stood under the pale fluorescent lights at the station and talked to Lance about the coroner's report. I'd pretended to focus on him, when what I really wanted was to grab the folder with its shiny seal from the St. James Parish coroner's office and run. "How'd he get our telephone number?"

"Your assistant must have given it to him."

Leave it to Beatrice to get to the shop at the crack of dawn. "Gotcha."

"Anyway, Lance wants to get together with you this morning," Ambrose said. "Told me you should meet him at the substation."

"Then I guess I should go. But let me finish my breakfast first. It's delicious, by the way."

Ambrose patted my knee as he rose. "Glad you like it. I'll be gone a few hours, so don't wait on me for anything. I've got a pretty big backload right now."

"That's because everyone wants to work with you, Bo. They all know you're the best."

"You must still be dreaming."

"No, I mean it." I set my fork on the tray. While I loved to tease him, I'd never kid Ambrose about his work. He could've chosen to stay in New York at a big-name fashion house, but he came down to the Great River Road instead. We were lucky to have him. "Isn't it time for you to hire some help? Yeah, you've got your seamstresses, but you need someone else. You can't keep working yourself to death."

"We'll see." He grinned and tapped his finger against his chin.

I took the hint and wiped some powdered sugar from my skin. "Thanks, darlin.' And don't forget to call me."

"Of course."

The minute he left the room, the delicious smell of his Armani cologne began to fade. I sighed and tucked back into my breakfast, missing him already.

Once I finished breakfast, I clamored out of bed and set the empty tray on the ground. My gaze flitted across the room to my closet, where a tangle of summer dresses, pastel polos, and capris tried to muscle each other out of the way. Poor things probably needed some fresh air.

It happened every wedding season. By August, my room looked like a hoarder's, and I could never find two shoes that matched.

I walked over and reached for a Lilly Pulitzer shift slanted on its hanger, which happened to be a personal favorite. After slipping into it, I headed for the bathroom, where I rubbed some concealer under my eyes, gathered my hair into a French twist, and brushed my teeth. Hopefully, I looked more respectable than I felt.

I yawned and ambled into the kitchen with my breakfast tray. I continued to yawn all the way to my car, while driving down the road and, finally, as I pulled into the parking lot of the police substation. By then I didn't even bother to cover my mouth.

Only two cars sat on the hot asphalt lot so early in the morning. Then again, it *was* a Tuesday, so maybe things were getting back to normal after a busy weekend.

I pulled up next to Lance's buggy squad car, walked around it, and then made my way into the building. Lance noticed me as soon as I arrived.

"Hey, there. You got my message." He stood next to the low counter, a navy splotch in a sea of beige.

"Yeah, Ambrose told me." Briskly, I rubbed my arms. "Heavens to Betsy. Why does it always feel like a meat locker in here?"

He chuckled. "You're complaining to the wrong guy. They set the temperature at headquarters." He pushed the secret button beneath the counter and the gate popped open. "C'mon back."

I followed him into the room, past file cabinets the color of warm toast and Formica desks dotted with cheap picture frames. A few crayoned drawings hung from the fabric walls; mostly stick figures with enormous heads and no feet.

Lance stopped behind one of the messier desks, of course. A slew of folders lay on its top, and darn if one of them didn't have the shiny foil seal of the St. James Parish coroner's office. It was different from the one I'd seen yesterday, though. *Here we go again.*

"I'll drive us to breakfast." Lance twirled a key ring in the air, obviously unaware of my wandering gaze.

"Uh?"

"Breakfast. I thought we'd get something to eat. My treat."

"Hmmm. I'd go with you, but I'm pretty full. Ambrose made me a stack of pancakes this morning."

Lance smirked. "Do tell."

"What? We're just friends. *Good* friends. He has his room and I have mine. Honestly. Get your mind out of the gutter."

"Whatever you say. Let's get going. You can have some coffee while I eat."

"Give me a minute." Casually, I pulled over a chair that belonged to a neighboring desk and sat. "Do you mind if we chat for a second first?"

Lance wouldn't bring the coroner's report with him to breakfast, and I was so curious about its contents I could've burst. I'd already burned holes in the cover with my staring.

"But I was kinda hoping to catch up with you," he said. "You know, talk about old times."

"Sure, we can do that. In a minute. By the way, I saw your mom last night."

Reluctantly, he sank into his desk chair. "All right, we'll do it your way. I'm not that hungry. How's my mom?"

"She's great. And her food was terrific." I eyed my old friend. "And I can chitchat with you about her restaurant until the cows come home. But you and I both know what I really want."

He followed my gaze to the folder, which lay between us. "I know. But just once I'd like to chat with you about something other than police work."

"We will. Once we start figuring out what happened to Mellette Babineaux. I promise."

He nodded at the report. "I know you're upset about it. But I can't figure why her murder has you so worked up. It's not like you two were family or anything."

"Yeah, she was family . . . in a way. She and I were sorority sisters back at Vanderbilt."

Lance dismissed the comment with a wave of his hand. "I wouldn't know about any of that stuff. Never got involved in that whole fraternity, sorority thing."

"Well, I got into it. They were like my sisters." My mind immediately reeled back to the faces of my pledge sisters, some of whom I hadn't seen in ten years. There was Darcy, who jogged ten miles every time she had a hangover, which ultimately earned her a spot on our school's track team. And Savannah, whose rich grandaddy flew her to South America every other weekend, while I scraped together quarters for Taco Bell. Or Blaire, who ended up owning an internet company and probably ruled half the world by now.

"Mellette Babineaux would have done the same thing for me."

"Okay, okay. Whatever you say. So you two were tight."

I shook my head to clear the memories. "Not tight, exactly. But I still feel like I owe her; like I should help her if I can. But I don't want to get you into trouble here."

"Don't worry, you won't." His hand stilled over the folder. "And if this is what you want . . . I have some bad news. The coroner didn't find anything."

"I *knew* that was an autopsy report. How'd they finish it so soon?"

"Rules say they've got twenty-four hours to write it once we've transported a body. But like I said, they didn't find any blunt-force trauma."

I remembered finding Mellette in the garden shed with Ambrose. Puddled under the windowsill in her business suit, which looked clean. "I believe it. She didn't look like she'd been attacked. But what about toxins?"

"That's the thing. We won't get a tox report back for six weeks or so, but the coroner's calling this one a negative autopsy."

"A *what*?"

"It means he didn't find anything wrong with the body. The ME did a good job too. I was there when he cracked her open."

"Eww." I scrunched up my nose.

"Sorry about that; but it's what we call it. The coroner checked her organs for damage. Nothing. Her heart looked good, her kidneys were fine. Then he checked her eyeballs."

"Her eyeballs?"

"For suffocation. The blood vessels behind 'em burst when there's no air. We call it *tiki eyes*."

"You guys have a weird sense of humor."

"Guess you get desensitized to it after a while." He exhaled loudly. "But she wasn't suffocated, either. Too bad I can't wave a magic wand over this-here report and come up with something more conclusive than that."

Lance's mention of magic wands spurred another memory. The night before, while driving home with Ambrose, we'd seen a pulsing light behind Sweetwater. It was an otherworldly bonfire, where a woman danced with a snake over her head before tossing it into the nearby woods.

"You need to know something," I said. "Ambrose and I stopped by Sweetwater after we left your mama's restaurant last night."

"Now why would you do that?" This time *he* looked put off. "That's a crime scene, Missy. You can't go running around there. You could've—"

"Hush a minute." Thank goodness we had such a long history together, so I knew he wouldn't take offense. "We happened to see something behind the house, so we stopped. Don't scowl at me like that. What'd you want us to do? Ignore a huge bonfire burning behind the property?"

Finally, he stopped grimacing.

"That's better. Anyway, we went around to the back to check out the light. Never thought we'd find a bunch of people there. This one gal had a poor snake over the fire, and she sang in something that sounded like Creole."

"You know that was a voodoo ceremony, right? They don't want strangers there. And it was probably Mother Belle you saw."

"I know all about her. Your mom told me. But there's more. I recognized one of the guys in the crowd. It was Hollis Oubre . . . Ruby's grandson."

"Now that's interesting." Lance's eyes narrowed. "He's on probation from juvie hall, so he's not supposed to be trespassing anywhere. Who else have you told?"

"No one. Well, no one but Ambrose."

"Good." Lance gave the coroner's report a slap. "Don't tell anyone else what happened at Sweetwater until I can talk to Ruby and Hollis. I don't want them to hear about it before I can get out to their place."

"Can I come too?"

He looked at me askance. "Now why'd you want to do that?"

"Ambrose recorded Mother Belle singing on his cell phone. I'd like to play it for Ruby. I'm pretty sure it was in Creole." I started to speak again, until I remembered something. "Rats! I need to stop by Ambrose's studio and get his phone back."

"I was gonna tell you no, but it might be interesting to see what that recording's all about." Lance reached for a telephone on his desk. "I'll tell you what . . . I'll try to get a search warrant for Miss Ruby's place, and you can come with me. But you gotta promise to behave."

"Scout's honor. And thanks." Finally, I relaxed enough to lean back. "Maybe we can finally get that cup of coffee when you're done with your call."

"No, this might take a while." He held the receiver in the air. "You can either sit tight or get something done in the meantime."

"Hmmm." Funny, but all of our talk about breakfast and such had made me want that cup of coffee more than ever. Especially since I'd only slept five hours or so, which wasn't nearly enough. "Okay. I'm gonna get some coffee. Do you want anything?"

"Thanks, but no thanks. I have to start this process so we can get out there this morning. I'll grab something later." He shot me a funny look. "The sooner you leave, the sooner I can start on this."

"Okay, okay. I can take a hint." I rose, my eyes still drawn to the folder on the desk. "Just once I wish you'd let me read a coroner's report without me having to beg for it."

"Maybe next time."

I made my way to the door, my shoulders shrinking under my thin cotton blouse. "And why don't you tell that headquarters of yours to turn the air-conditioning off in here while you're at it?" I threw the words over my shoulder. "I'm frozen solid."

I turned to see him roll his eyes. Yes, we most certainly had a history together.

Chapter 9

My shoulders began to relax the minute I stepped into bright sun-shine. I made my way to the car, yanked the door open, and sat on the warmed driver's seat. A quick glance at the dash told me it was 8:30 and already edging up to 85 degrees. *Welcome to summer in the South.* Where a girl could freeze one minute and melt the next.

I pulled away from the lot and headed for the highway. Traffic was blessedly light today, and I had no problem merging into a lane. Normally I had to negotiate my way around a swaying oil tanker with its grinding gears, jostling axles, and squeaking air brakes.

Within minutes, I'd pulled off the road and arrived at my destina-tion. Dippin' Donuts had the best coffee in town, not to mention the quirkiest atmosphere. It was housed in a 1950s bungalow topped by a giant neon sign shaped like an arrow. *TASTY D-LITES*, read the shaft. Also attached to the roof was a striped metal awning that stretched over a drive-through lane that no one ever used, since everyone came to the doughnut shop for the conversation as much as the crullers.

Once Grady, the owner, had bought the place, he pretty much left it alone and eventually stopped tugging at the weeds that appeared in the cracks between the drive-through's concrete.

A handful of cars sat on the lot today, including Grady's two-tone pickup. What caught my eye, though, was an enormous sedan that straddled two parking spaces near the entrance. Sleek as a Gulf-stream jet, its hood gently inclined as it offered up a hood ornament of a winged woman poised for flight. I knew at a glance who owned it. But whatever could Herbert Solomon be doing at Dippin' Donuts on a Tuesday morning?

I parked near the Rolls and scooted around its massive hood on my way into the bakery. The aroma of fried dough, sugar frosting, and coffee grounds greeted me as I entered.

Grady stood behind the display case this morning, wearing a white apron and a sleeveless T-shirt that showed off his tattoos. His elbows rested on the glass, which showed off the newest one: a giant whisk on his right bicep.

"Hey, Grady." I walked up to him and he straightened.

"Hi, Missy."

Somehow he made the ordinary chef's apron look sexy. Even though he definitely wasn't my type—my type being big-city boys like Ambrose—he *did* have a charming smile and those toned biceps. "Got any coffee left?"

"Think I do." He turned and pulled a carafe from the Bunn machine. "You're in luck. I still have half a pot." He swirled the carafe a few times before pouring some into a Styrofoam cup and passing it to me.

"All the coffee drinkers must be at work already." I smiled and rummaged through my pocket for change.

"Don't worry about it." He waved my efforts away. "It's on the house. If you don't mind my saying . . . you look kinda rough this morning. Late night?"

I groaned. "Is it that obvious? Maybe I should have used more Maybelline concealer."

"No, it's not obvious." He seemed to regret having made the remark. "But your eyes look tired." He grabbed a paper sack and ducked behind the case. When he reappeared, the sack bulged with doughnut holes. "Here . . . my treat. Didn't mean to insult you."

"I know you didn't." I willingly accepted his offering, even though Ambrose had spoiled me rotten with breakfast not long before. At this rate I was going to be fatter than a tick if I didn't watch out.

"You never did answer my question, though," he said. "Anything wrong?"

"Just a lot on my mind. Speaking of which—" I glanced over my shoulder. Sure enough, Herbert Solomon had unfurled a sheath of papers on a back table and was pouring over them. "What's Mr. Solomon doing here? It's hard to miss him with that big ol' car of his."

"True." He jerked his head at the billionaire. "He's been here all morning. Brought in some blueprints and hasn't budged."

My smile faded. No doubt he'd brought blueprints for Sweetwater.

"Missy?"

"Excuse me, but I've gotta take care of something." I fished a dollar from my pocket and shoved it into the tip jar before Grady could stop me. "I'll be right back."

While I felt like dashing over to Herbert Solomon and ripping away the blueprints, I took my sweet time sashaying over to his table, where I stopped. "Why, hello there."

He glanced up. "Hello."

"What a nice surprise." I hoped my smile didn't look too forced. "Is Ivy here too?"

"No, she stayed home."

"Mind if I have a seat, then?" I quickly sat and placed the coffee cup next to me on the laminate bench. "Don't you look busy this morning. What *is* all this?"

"Obviously, they're blueprints."

I ignored the condescending tone. "You don't say. You and your wife must be planning a big remodel."

"Hell, no. We did that last year. Nearly bankrupted me."

Since my chitchat was getting us nowhere, I casually held up the bag of doughnut holes. "Want one?" Maybe the fried balls of dough would loosen his tongue.

"Sure." He reached across the table and plucked a doughnut hole from the bag, which he popped into his mouth.

"Grady's a whiz with these," I said. "Here. Have another."

This time he pulled two from the sack. "Don't mind if I do." He shoved them both in his mouth and began to chew. He might be worth a billion dollars, but he also smacked his lips something awful.

Bless his heart. "So . . . what are the blueprints for?"

He finally swallowed. "I'm trying to buy another plantation around here. One that'll work as apartments. High-end, you know."

"That so." My cheeks began to warm, even though Grady kept the air in here so low it reminded me of the police station.

"But I need to make a few changes first," he said. "Place needs a new entrance and a parking lot out front."

Lorda mercy. "All that at Sweetwater?"

"Yeah. How'd you know that's the place I'm talking about?"

"I was there yesterday morning too. Remember?"

"Now I do. That's when I couldn't find the goddamn real estate agent."

"And the property just came on the market." The image of a bull-dozer clawing at tree roots ran through my mind. "How'd you get the plans drawn up so quickly?"

"Trust me. I know all about the plantations around here. I've been interested in that one for a long time." His eyes narrowed. "Wait a minute. Don't tell me you want to buy that place too?"

"Who ... me?" I pretended to be shocked. "There's no way I could afford it." A little white lie never hurt anyone, especially since we both knew he could buy and sell me ten times over. "But I thought you didn't tour it yesterday. You never know. Some of the rooms could be a wreck." Of course they weren't, but that was nei-ther here nor there at this point.

"Doesn't matter. All of those places need remodeling anyway. The rooms are never big enough and the walls have that godawful paneling. Don't even get me started on the useless antiques. Nothing a complete reno can't fix."

Dawg nabbit ... he's put some thought into this. "But don't you need to get changes like that approved by the National Registry of Historic Places?" Surely they wouldn't let him destroy a hundred-year-old live oak or a beautiful mahogany panel.

"Funny you should say that." He smirked, as if he knew I wouldn't find it the least bit funny. "No one ever bothered to get historic status for that house. The registry can't force private owners, you know."

My cheeks flamed even more. *He was right.* It was all voluntary. People applied for historic status because they wanted to preserve a house. Sometimes for the bragging rights and sometimes after pres-sure from neighbors and friends. "But there must be a local planning board."

"Sure, there's that. But the city's planning commission is in a mess right now. One of their directors died yesterday."

"Died?"

"Some Realtor. Helluva time for it to happen."

The sounds of the bakery began to fade as his words sunk in. Could it be possible? Did Mellette serve on the planning commission before she died? Come to think of it, it *did* make perfect sense. Planning commissions usually included builders, inspectors, and real-estate agents. "You must be talking about Mellette Babineaux."

"Who the hell's that?"

"The Realtor for Sweetwater. Her name was right there on the sales flyer."

"I don't waste my time reading those things." He puffed out his cheeks. "It's all advertising, anyway."

"But—"

"Look, Miss DuBois. I've got a busy day ahead of me. Nice to see you again." He dismissed me with a nod.

I slowly rose, knowing he wouldn't say anything more. "Nice to see you too."

Somehow I made my way to the counter without spilling my coffee. Grady stared at me. "What'd he say to you?"

"Huh? What?" I barely felt the weight of the cup in my hand.

"What did he say?"

"Nothing." I took a sip of the lukewarm coffee to buy myself some time. No need to get into a windy conversation with Grady about Sweetwater. He'd only tell me to forget about the property, like everyone else had done.

"You don't look like he said nothing. I'm gonna go over there and give that guy a piece of my mind—"

"No." I shook my head. "It's okay. He just told me some disturbing news, that's all. No big deal."

Grady wouldn't let it drop, though. "I still think something's up. What'd he say?"

"Look . . . Mr. Solomon's trying to buy Sweetwater. He wants to turn it into high-end apartments. Thinks he can do anything he wants because the planning commission's a mess right now."

"He said that? That doesn't make sense. The commission gave me so much stuff to do when I bought this place, it was crazy. We're talking checklists and legal forms and so many phone calls I stopped answering 'em. That's why I left everything here the same."

That would explain the cheesy neon sign outside and the drive-through lane that no one ever used.

"But there's more. You know about Mellette Babineaux, right?"

"Of course," he said. "Everyone knows."

"I met her yesterday, when I went to see the property."

"You went to Sweetwater? You're not thinking—"

"Hold on." My granddaddy always said the best defense was a good offense. "I know what people say about the place. That it's haunted. They practice voodoo there. And now there's been a murder. But I tell you, Grady, it's the prettiest thing I've ever seen. It's got a shed out back that would make a perfect design studio."

When he didn't reply, I shrugged. "Aren't you gonna say anything?"

"I get it. I really do. The house is nice to look at. But a lot of people won't go near it. That should tell you something."

"But you told me this building was filthy when you bought it. People probably told you to walk away from it, but you didn't. Mr. Solomon wants to tear down the old oaks on the front lawn and pave right over the grass."

"He said that?"

"Well, not exactly. But if he wants to add a parking lot, he's gonna have to tear down the trees. Course I told him he'd never get away with it. But there's more. No one ever applied for historic status for that house."

"That would've been the Coxes' job. They owned it for a long time."

"I know. I met one of their sons—Ashley—yesterday."

Grady grimaced. "He's supposed to be a little shit. That's what everyone around here says, anyway. Him and his brother went to some fancy schools back East."

"I think Ashley went to Yale."

"Whatever. It might as well have been Mars to hear people around here tell it. They say the kids didn't come back until their parents died. And then only to get the money."

"Interesting." That would explain the expensive Rolex. "Anyway, Mellette Babineaux was the real estate agent there. And apparently on the local planning commission."

Before I could say more, a little girl wearing turquoise cowboy boots wiggled her way between me and the doughnut case.

"'Scuse me." She pointed to a doughnut on the lowest shelf. "Can I have a chocolate sprinkle, please?"

Grady bent to retrieve it. "Sure, darlin.' Now don't eat it too fast." He winked after he'd straightened and handed her the doughnut. "You'll give yourself a bellyache."

"Thanks." She stuck out her arm and handed him a dollar.

While Grady made change, I glanced at the clock behind him. "Look, I shouldn't even bother you while you're working. Thanks for the coffee. And for the doughnut holes."

"No problem." He doled out the little girl's change. "And don't let Mr. Solomon get to you. That one's slicker than snot."

I couldn't help but grin. Now *there* was an expression Ambrose would never use. "See you later."

I began to walk away, mulling over my conversation with Herbert Solomon. Unfortunately, everything he'd said made perfect sense. Why wouldn't Mellette be on the planning commission? She sold real estate. And any commissioner's death would throw a group like that into chaos for at least a few weeks. Long enough for someone like him to push through a remodeling plan.

And what about his attitude? The billionaire didn't seem too concerned with Mellette's death. If anything, he seemed grateful for the distraction, as if she'd done him a favor by dying.

I swung open the plate-glass door and stepped outside. Bright sun glanced off the windshields of the few cars that remained, especially the oversized Rolls. I slowed as I walked past it on my way to my car.

The exterior glowed. Even the statue on the grille looked liquid. I peered through the passenger window, wondering if it was possible for the inside to look as nice. There, on the front seat, right next to his day planner, lay a sales flyer for Sweetwater. The same flyer he claimed he'd never seen. Apparently, he not only had a copy, but he'd circled the price in black pen, which meant he'd studied the thing. Why did he lie?

I leaned away from the window. It was such a small thing, really. He should've admitted to knowing Mellette Babineaux was the Realtor for Sweetwater, but he didn't.

I ambled over to my car and swung open the door. As soon as I plopped onto the driver's seat, the cell in my pocket jangled. I pulled it out and wedged it between my shoulder and chin as I started the car. "Hello?"

"Hi, Missy. It's me."

I hadn't spoken to Beatrice since yesterday. She didn't know I'd gone to Sweetwater with Ambrose, and that we'd seen an actual voodoo ceremony. "Thank God you called, Bea. You won't believe what Ambrose and I—"

"Uh, Missy?" Her voice was strained. "It might have to wait. We have a little . . . um . . . situation on our hands."

I quickly took the phone away from my shoulder while the car idled. "What do you mean . . . situation?"

"One of the brides—" Before she could say more, a crack sounded as her phone smacked against something hard. She must have laid it on the counter.

"Beatrice? You pick up your phone right now!"

Thankfully, she came back on the line. "Sorry about that. You've got to get back to the studio, Missy." Her voice sounded tight; not like the Beatrice I knew.

"Why? What's wrong?"

"Just a second." Another crack as she laid the phone down again.

"Stop doing that! Get back on the line right now!"

"I'm back." She whispered into the receiver. "One of your brides came in this morning and she's screaming bloody murder."

"First things first. Who is it, and what's the problem?"

"Jennalee Prudhomme. The one who's getting married on the *Dixie Queen*."

My stomach lurched. I'd met several bridezillas in my day, but Jennalee took the cake. She'd arrived at our first appointment with a year's worth of *Modern Bride* magazines and dissected each and every wedding photo from top to bottom. It took her almost two hours to do that, which was when I realized that time meant nothing to her. At least not other people's time.

"Sugar! What's wrong now? Let me guess . . . her white lace isn't white enough."

"Worse." Bea's voice dropped even lower. "Turns out she went to a wedding this weekend. Guess what the bride was wearing?"

"Please don't tell me she had the same type of hat."

In the end, Jennalee had picked a flower and lace fascinator with a birdcage veil. The Alençon lace came from Switzerland and Swarovski made the crystals for the veil. The whole thing ended up costing a thousand dollars, which she happily charged to her daddy's credit card.

"How can that be?"

"She said it was an exact match. Brought hers in here and dumped it on the floor. Thought she was gonna have a temper tantrum right in the middle of the store."

I ran my hand across my eyes. "Sounds like she's lost it."

"She wants to see you too. Said she would've come yesterday, but the family's jet wasn't available. How quick can you get here?"

I thought about lying and pretending to be in a meeting, but only for a second. Instead, I glanced at the clock on my dash. "It's a little after ten. Tell her I'll be there in five minutes."

"Okay. But if she tries to hold her breath, I might have to throttle her."

Chapter 10

Of course, a convoy of tanker trucks clogged the highway since I was in a hurry now. A slow-moving Peterbilt, a water-spray truck, and a shiny Liquid Transport freightliner all lumbered along beside me and wedged me in, but I made it to the off-ramp anyway and whizzed past the retaining wall.

Soon the parking lot for the Factory appeared. Apparently there was a problem here too, since a line of cars waited to enter. I pulled in behind a tiny Smart car and fiddled with the air-conditioner until it was my turn. When I reached the front of the line, the problem became obvious: a candy-apple red Mercedes had blocked the loading zone and forced everyone else to swerve around it on their way in.

I finally veered around the troublemaking Benz and cruised the lot for a few minutes until I found a parking space. Then I hurried to Crowning Glory and paused to catch my breath in front of the studio's window.

On the other side of the glass Jennalee Prudhomme, with a high ponytail and skintight blue jeans, stood with Beatrice by the cash register. She stomped her foot a few times, and the sole of her Christian Louboutin pump flashed red like a warning sign. She didn't seem to notice she'd almost smashed the expensive fascinator that now lay on the ground.

I plastered a smile on my face and swung open the door. "Hello, there." I casually walked to the counter, scooping up the fascinator at the same time.

Jennalee wheeled on me. "Well, well, well. Did we wake you?"

Little does she know I've been up for hours. "I'm sorry, but I had some business in town. I understand you're not happy with your order?"

"Look at it!" She pointed at the hat, the diamond ring on her left hand flashing. It was three carats, at least, or about as much as I paid to rent the studio for an entire year. "How am I supposed to wear this thing when every other girl in Louisiana has the same one?"

Beatrice opened her mouth until I shot her a warning look. Of course Jennalee was exaggerating, but pointing it out would only make things worse. Much better to catch flies with honey than with vinegar, as my granddaddy would say.

"There, there. Let's see what we can do."

I escorted Jennalee through the studio and over to a pair of comfy armchairs in the back. I'd slipcovered the plump cushions in white taffeta and hung a dainty chandelier above our heads. Beside the chairs was a carved armoire that held hair combs, pearls, and silk stockings; its doors closed by a beautiful antique tassel spun from glass and layered in velvet.

Many times I'd tried to close up shop for the night, only to find a bridesmaid or two napping in the homey sitting area.

Unfortunately, Jennalee did *not* look sleepy. She perched on the edge of her armchair with her legs crossed. "I was so mortified, I coulda' died."

I subtly nodded to Beatrice as I sat, who retreated to the break room to grab a water bottle for our guest. "We'll get you some water. Now, I understand another bride had your exact design. I must say I was surprised, since yours was a custom order."

Jennalee wouldn't look at me. Instead, she eyed the chandelier, the chairs, the curio cabinet . . . anything but me and her very expensive hat. "I know. That's what I thought. Couldn't believe it when I saw it coming down the aisle." She sniffled. "Course I didn't see any flowers on hers. Or that lace stuff on the front. And maybe it was a lot shorter. But other than that, it was an exact match! Which your little helper didn't seem to think was such a problem."

Thankfully, Beatrice hadn't emerged from the break room yet, and she couldn't hear Jennalee. When she finally reappeared a few seconds later, she passed me a water bottle, which I gave to Jennalee.

"Here. Let's see what we can do."

The girl unscrewed the cap and chugged from the bottle as I held the fascinator to the light. Come to think of it, I should've asked Beatrice to bring a fifth of Jack Daniel's instead of Aquafina.

All the while, the fascinator sparkled prettily in my hand, like a starburst twinkling under the light. Instead of simple netting, I'd used Alençon lace dusted with Swarovski Wild Heart crystals and then added silk roses at the crown. I'd cut and pleated each rose petal using silk *habatoi*, which took the better part of a day, if I recalled correctly. The finishing touch was a cascade of *coque* and hackle feathers that drifted downward.

"It's got to be perfect," Jennalee said. "Otherwise, I'll be the laughingstock of the country club."

My mind swirled as I appraised the hat. I'd run up against something similar in the not-so-distant past. Only then I'd held a hat under the harsh glare of a spotlight while technicians swirled around me as they adjusted rigging for a fashion show. Models with makeup kits and garment bags whooshed by me in the memory. Even now my heart raced when I thought about it.

The whole thing had started on a whim. I'd visited a local church near Morningside Plantation the morning after my bride was found murdered there. The church desperately needed money, and since Ambrose and I suddenly had free time on our hands, we volunteered to produce a fashion show. Or—as Ambrose liked to remind me—I volunteered us to produce a fashion show . . . with less than thirty hours to spare.

Somehow, it all fell into place, until the garment bags arrived that night and I realized my favorite hat had gone missing. I'd reserved it for the big finale and the newspaper's photographs afterward, which meant I'd have to rework one of the other hats now.

Sometime between the start of the fashion show and the closing number, I was forced to create a masterpiece using only what I could scrounge up backstage.

Never one to panic, Ambrose had helped me by intercepting one of the first models after she strutted the runway. He plucked the hat from her head the minute she walked past the curtain, and then he passed it to me with a wink. "Do your magic."

And I did. With only a pair of scissors, a yard of iridescent taffeta, and a handful of compacts from the models' makeup kits, I created a design worthy of a center spread in *Stylist Magazine*, if I did say so myself.

First, I gathered the taffeta into dozens of tiny tassels. Then I splintered the mirrors I'd found in the compacts and glued the shards between the folds of fabric. I took extra care to glue fabric all around the bits of mirrors, so as not to scratch the model's face.

The minute she stepped under the stage lights, the tassels glittered as if showered with snowflakes. The audience began to murmur about the design, which was simple, yet stunning.

My eyes traveled to Jennalee now and then to the armoire behind her. *Of course.* I rose and silently walked to the cabinet. But instead of opening the doors, I unwound the heavy glass-and-velvet tassel that bound the handles.

I'd spied the trimming in the window at Keil's Antiques in New Orleans. It'd cost a fortune, but the salesperson explained it once belonged in an eighteenth-century salon in Paris.

I sank into the armchair with the hat and the tassel now, back in my studio. Beatrice seemed to read my mind, because she brought over some hatpins and Sticky Tack we kept at the front counter, and all the while Jennalee kept talking.

"Your dress is a sweetheart neckline, right?" I asked, once she finally paused for breath. At the same time, I pinned the tassel's cord to a comb hidden under the headpiece.

"Yeah, it is." Jennalee sniffled again. "A Pnina Tornai. Custom-made and everything."

When I finished temporarily securing the tassel, I took a handful of glass beads we kept in a bowl for decoration and began to layer them into the headband, using Sticky Tack to hold them in place for now.

I could feel Jennalee's eyes on the top of my head as I bent over the hat. When I finished attaching the beads, I flipped the tassel forward and turned to face her. The antique tassel exploded with tiny bursts of light when it caught the reflection of the chandelier.

"It's *sooo* pretty." Jennalee breathed the words.

"And the tassel's from the 1700s," I said. "A French baron owned it." Now, that may or may not have been the truth, but my fib seemed to work, because Jennalee's eyes grew to three times their normal size.

"Gorgeous!" She grabbed the hat out of my hands and raced to a three-sided mirror on the wall. After ripping out her ponytail holder, she jammed the fascinator into place. "I love it! I have to have it."

My shoulders relaxed. I'd managed to tame another bridezilla using a bit of fabric, a touch of sparkle, and a dash of imagination. "I'm so glad you like it."

"Finally, something's gone right. You wouldn't believe the nonsense I've had to put up with." Jennalee swished her head this way and that as she spoke, the tassel brushing her cheek each time. "Just last month I got a call about my reception. Can you believe it? Last month!"

"You're having it on the *Dixie Queen*, right?"

"Yes, indeed. But they had the nerve to call and ask if I'd mind sharing it for the evening." Finally satisfied, she glanced away from the mirror. "They wanted me to loan the downstairs to some stupid auction house around here for the night. Of course, I told them no."

That caught Beatrice's attention. "Hey . . . I've heard about that auction house. Don't they sell antiques on the deck of the riverboat? Really cool ones too."

Jennalee didn't answer at first, since she was so busy fingering the tassel's fringe. "They could sell off the Statue of Liberty for all I care. I'm not gonna share that riverboat with anyone. It's like the devil himself is trying to ruin my big day!"

"You poor thing," I murmured.

After tossing her head a final time, Jennalee reluctantly whisked off the fascinator and handed it to me. "How soon can you sew everything in place?"

"I'll start on it now. Is that soon enough?"

"Perfect. And I have a new magazine in my car for me and this one to read." She jerked her head to Beatrice. "I'll just run out to my Benz and get it. Won't take me but a second since I got the best parking space in the whole lot."

Of course . . . the candy-apple red Mercedes in the loading zone. I should've expected as much.

It took me an hour to restructure the fascinator to carry the weight of the tassel. When I finished, I emerged from the workroom and presented it to Jennalee with a flourish. "There you go. You'll be the belle of the ball."

She had trapped Beatrice in the sitting area with her bridal magazine and Beatrice looked ready to kiss me on the spot. I made a mental note to pay her time-and-a-half on her next paycheck for the pain and suffering.

Praise the Lord, we'd soon be free of Jennalee. I gently wrapped her fascinator in acid-free tissue, placed it in a hatbox, and gave it to her. Then I guided her to the front door with my hand firmly on her elbow. We'd almost made it too, when Beatrice spoke up.

"You never told us what happened with the auction. Did they cancel it?"

"What?" Jennalee stopped, and the hatbox banged against her thigh. "Think they're gonna have it at someone's office around here. To be honest, I couldn't care less as long as they don't have it on my riverboat."

I held the door open for her and she sailed out. The bang of the door behind her sounded downright heavenly.

"Hallelujah. She's gone."

"That one's a piece of work." Beatrice leaned over the counter as she paged through our calendar for the week. "But your solution was brilliant."

"I copied it from one of my other designs." I wandered back to the counter, the tension leeching from my shoulders. "Back then I used shredded fabric for the fringe."

"Whatever it takes." Beatrice glanced down again. She'd scribbled notes on the margins of the calendar; a jumble of letters, dollar signs, and doodles. "You got some calls while that one was yakking away. Don't think she even realized I took 'em while she was talking. Most of them were salespeople, but you got a few important ones too. Vinnie said to tell you he mailed the organza you wanted. He's sorry about the delay." She looked at her notes again. "And a cop called and said he's a friend of yours. Something about a search warrant this afternoon. What's that all about?"

To be honest, I'd forgotten about Lance. I vaguely remembered telling him I wanted to visit Ruby Oubre's house again, but that seemed like ages ago. "His name is Lance LaPorte. I'll tell you about it after I call him back."

"You might want to get something to eat first. You look kinda pale."

Why does everyone insist on telling me that? First Grady, who made up for the comment with doughnut holes, and now Beatrice. "You're the second person who's told me I look bad. Can't a girl lose a little sleep around here without everyone noticing?"

"Sorry. Didn't mean to hurt your feelings. Let me get you a sandwich or something."

"Okay. But nothing messy, please. I'll have to eat it in the car on my way to the police station."

"You got it. The bakery opens at eleven."

Beatrice went back to studying our schedule, and I pulled out my cell and dialed Lance's number.

He answered on the first ring. "Hi, Missy. You musta got my message."

"Uh-huh. I was dealing with a bridezilla. What's up?"

"They came through with a search warrant for Ruby Oubre's place. You still want to go with me?"

I checked the digital clock on the cash register. It was almost eleven, so the heat and humidity would be at full throttle. "Guess so." At least I'd worn brown flats today that would hide the Louisiana mud. "Good thing I'm not wearing sandals."

"I don't care what you wear, as long as you let me do most of the talking."

"No problem. But yesterday I went out there in a white skirt and strappy sandals. Not gonna make that mistake again."

He chuckled. "You're a hot mess."

"What killed me was getting in and out of that dang boat."

"Boat?"

"Yeah . . . we took a pirogue. Borrowed the thing from Beatrice's uncle." My voice swelled with pride. "It was my first time out in one. Did pretty good, if I do say so myself."

Instead of congratulating me like I thought he would, Lance burst out laughing.

"What's so funny?" I glanced over at Beatrice, who pretended to study the calendar, although I knew she was eavesdropping on us.

"Don't you know there's a service road out there? It's used by the fire department. Heck, I haven't boated on the Atchafalaya in years. Lord knows what kind of creatures live in that water."

"Really." I arched an eyebrow at Beatrice. "You don't say. How very interesting. Will you excuse me a minute?"

I cupped my hand over the receiver. Although it was nice of her uncle to loan us the boat, the ride had ruined my skirt and my favorite pair of strappy sandals. Not to mention I'd lost about a pound of water weight in sweat. I hardened my voice. "Beatrice Rushing."

She looked at me and gulped.

"Lance tells me there's a fire road that leads out to Miss Ruby's house. We didn't have to take your uncle's boat out there after all."

"Oops." But instead of looking contrite like she should have, the little devil actually grinned. "Guess that makes sense. But it was kinda fun watching you struggle out there."

"Why, you little—"

"Missy?"

I moved my hand away from the telephone receiver. "Sorry, Lance. Turns out my assistant was having some fun with me yesterday on the river."

"Uh-oh. I wouldn't do that if I were her."

"She doesn't know me like you do. Her time will come."

Beatrice buried her head farther into the calendar and pretended to not hear me.

"So, let's get going," Lance said. "We can take my squad car. And don't be too hard on your assistant. The last thing we need around here is another murder. See you soon."

"Guess so. Bye." I hung up the telephone and turned to Beatrice. "All right, smarty-pants. We'll talk about this later. Right now I need to get Ambrose's cell phone and head out to the police station." I quickly filled her in on everything that'd happened to me and Bo the night before. "Call me if anything comes up."

"Yes, ma'am."

She hadn't called me "ma'am" in ages, so my comments must have spooked her. I grabbed the keys to Ringo and headed for the exit. Luckily, Ambrose was in his studio and tossed me his cell phone without a word.

Chapter 11

Imade it to the police station in record time and quickly parked next to Lance's squad car. Then I hurried across the parking lot and entered the lobby.

A blast of frigid air greeted me as soon as I stepped inside.

Lance was across the room, near a beige file cabinet, and he walked toward me when I arrived "Good, you're here. That didn't take long."

"Traffic was a breeze. By the way, how'd you get a search warrant so fast?"

"The courthouse clerk and I are friends. Didn't take long for the judge to sign the affidavit. Especially since we've been out to Ruby's place before."

"You mentioned that. Are you ready to go?"

"In a minute. I want to phone my captain and tell him where I am."

Goose bumps prickled my arms. "I'll wait outside. It's too dang cold in here. Are we taking the squad car?"

"No . . . let's take my car. Don't want to spook Miss Ruby. It's the tan Olds in the last row." He tossed me his car keys.

"Got it. See you outside."

A guy wearing maroon scrubs held the door open for me as I emerged from the police station. I spotted Lance's Buick in the last row, behind a sleek BMW, which made his car look even worse by comparison.

Dust covered everything but a fan-shaped imprint on the front window, which the wipers had somehow scraped clean.

I peered through the smeared passenger window before opening the car. A crumpled bag of Cheetos shared the seat with a stack of papers and an empty 7-Eleven Big Gulp. *Does Odilia LaPorte know about her son's sloppiness?*

With a sigh, I opened the door and swept my hand along the seat to knock off the trash. By the time I'd settled in, Lance had appeared, and I pointed to the bag of Cheetos on the floorboard as he stepped into the car. "Breakfast?"

"Don't knock it 'til you've tried it. It's got cheese, right?" He took the keys from me and started the car.

"What's that smell?"

"Probably my sneakers," he said. "I left my gym bag in the back-seat."

"I swaney . . . this thing is a piece of work."

"Anyway . . ." he obviously hoped to change the subject, "let's go over how we're gonna do this. I'll show Ruby the judge's order and explain why we're there. That is, if she's home."

"She should be. She was there yesterday when Beatrice and I went out. She might not know what her grandson does for fun, though."

Lance pulled out of the parking lot and headed for Highway 975. As we crossed the first bridge, the tupelo cypresses once again appeared, like ghostly sentinels wearing thin sheets of moss. Several more miles later, we passed the spot where the tupelos parted naturally and the water rose up to meet the riverbank. It was the same bank from which we'd launched the pirogue yesterday.

Lance scanned the canopy as he drove. I tried to study the scenery too, but my eyes grew heavy and I leaned my head against the window, despite the smudgy fingerprints and streaks of dirt now rubbing into my hair. After a few minutes I nodded off, while warm air blew across my forehead and the wind whooshed in my ears. Without warning, Lance made a hard right and I jerked awake.

We were on a bumpy service road that ran perpendicular to the river. Gravel crunched beneath the Buick's tires, and the axle groaned whenever we hit a particularly bad bump.

At one point, the cypresses parted again and the river appeared. Like before, debris from the trees covered its surface until the water looked thick enough to walk on. Egrets swooped overhead, their slender necks sometimes parallel to the webbed clumps of hydrilla below.

We continued to drive, until smaller paths began to fork off from the service road like fingers reaching into the trees. An orange mail-box appeared, and then another box for the *Times-Picayune*.

Lance seemed to know his way around as he automatically turned at a lightning-scarred tree. We drove closer to the river until we reached the mobile home on cinder blocks and the listing dock, al-though I couldn't quite tell whether a dog was lying in wait for us there.

What I *did* see was a blue Chevy Nova with its windows rolled down and a paint job long ago faded by the sun. "Looks like she's home."

Lance pulled up alongside the Chevy. "Just hope she's in the mood to talk."

We stepped out of the car and onto hardened mud. The only sound was our footfalls on the dirt. About halfway to the house, I spied a small flower bed, of all things, tucked behind a rotting doghouse. Someone had edged the messy plot with chicken wire to keep the river animals away, and then planted some strange-looking flowers I couldn't identify.

A noise sounded from inside the home. Ruby was at the screen door, wearing a polka-dotted housecoat and tattered bedroom slip-pers.

"Miss Ruby." Lance waved the search warrant as he approached her. "We'd like to come in and talk to you for a bit."

She clenched a brown cigarette between her teeth, which she slowly withdrew. "Why? Dere's nothin' ta find here. Musta been a slow mornin' for ya."

Lance chuckled. "Not really. But I'm working on the Mellette Babineaux murder. Look, it's a hundred degrees out here. Mind if we step inside?"

"No skin of'n ma nose." She jerked her head back. "Put da dog up already."

I followed Lance into the dark mobile home. All sunlight stopped at the threshold, which left only murky, gray light to navigate by. The living room smelled of dust, burned tobacco, and fried hash browns.

Little by little, my eyes detected the hazy outline of the couch with its pile of old newspapers and Dollar General bags. I walked to-ward it but chose to lean against the armrest instead, since I didn't like my odds of finding a bare spot between the newspapers and plastic bags.

"Where's yer gris-gris?" Ruby studied me from her spot near the kitchen.

"Sorry . . . I forgot it back at my rent house, on the kitchen table," I said. "Thank you, by the way."

"It ain't gonna do ya no good der. I done tole ya ta keep 'er close."

"I know, but I forgot. And what were the chicken bones for?"

"Dey's special cuz dey's crossed. Keep da bad spirits away. Everbody 'round here knows dat." She rolled her eyes as she took a quick puff from her cigarette.

"We're here to ask you about something else." Lance seemed impatient with our small talk. "Something about Sweetwater."

"I tole dis one everytin' I know." She jerked her head at me. "Nutin' more ta say."

"Here's the thing. Melissa saw something last night you should be aware of."

"It was Hollis," I said. My granddaddy always did tell me the best way to get at the truth was to up and ask for it, and I had nothing left to lose. "Is he here with you?"

"Hollis? Dat's wot dis is about? Wot dat boy done now?"

"We're not sure, Miss Ruby. Is he here?" I repeated.

"Don' know. Ain't seen 'em dis morning.'"

"We'd like to check." Lance held up the search warrant. "And see his room."

"Ya ain't tole me wot he's done."

I suddenly remembered the cell phone in my pocket, which Ambrose had loaned me. "We're not sure yet. Did he say anything about going to a voodoo ceremony last night?"

"Ya be talkin' 'bout dat Mother Belle, *n'est-ce pas*?"

"Yep. 'Fraid so," Lance said. "She's back to doing her stuff over at Sweetwater. Do you know anything?"

"Nah, I don' got time fer dat."

"Hollis was there. I saw him in the back. Everyone was singing a strange song. My friend recorded it." I pulled the phone out of my pocket. "Listen." When I pushed the *playback* button, a reedy soprano began to sing:

Ena! Ena!
Akout, Akout an deye
Jocomo fi nou wa na né
Jockomo fi na né

Ruby slowly took the cigarette away from her lips as the song came to an end, and her eyes fluttered closed. "Was she wearin' dat snake again?"

I nodded, although she couldn't see me. "She was. Almost threw it in the fire until she changed her mind."

"Hah!" Her eyes flew open. "Dat's all for show. Weren't no way she gonna ruin da good snake. Dat song ain't even voodoo. She stole if from da black Indians up in Naw'leans."

"Black Indians?" I glanced sideways at Lance.

"There used to be tribes up there," he said. "Everyone a mix of African-American and Native American. All these people speaking pidgin French. They learned it from French slave masters who came down the Mississippi."

"But what does it mean?" I asked.

Ruby shrugged, which sent ashes spiraling to the linoleum. "It's da war cry. Makes people wanna fight. Nowadays da krewes in Naw'leans sing it, but dey jus' playactin'."

Since I still didn't understand why a voodoo queen would use an old war cry, I moved closer to the kitchen to be near Ruby. "Why would Mother Belle and her people want to fight?"

"Dat's a good question. Dey coulda been celebratin' too."

"Did your grandson tell you he was going there?" Lance asked. "They were at Sweetwater around midnight."

"Nah. He don' tell me nuthin'."

"So you didn't hear him come home?" Lance was an expert at knowing when to press and when to back off.

"I tol' you. I didn't hear nothin'. Dat boy be ro-day, is what dey call it. Cain't stay home."

"But he's homeschooled," I said. "Seems to me he should be doing his studying right about now."

She stiffened. I'd hit a sore spot, but it was too late to take it back.

"Ya from da gov'ment? Wanna turn in ma boy?"

Ambrose always did tell me my mouth moved faster than my brain and the last thing I wanted to do was get on Ruby's bad side.

"No, no. Of course not. But I thought you might have seen him come home last night. Or seen him this morning."

She was about to lash out at me again when something sounded from a back room. Something high and loud. *Skkkrrriiitttccchhh.*

Ruby turned. "*Tais-toi*, Jack!"

The noise stopped. Three rooms branched off of the hall behind her. I took a stab at which one she'd yelled at. "Do you let him stay in your bedroom?"

"Nah, he ain't ma dog. He belong to Hollis. I done tol' dat boy . . ."

Cccrrraaassshhh! A door flew open and the dog whizzed past us. It barreled toward Lance with its teeth bared and then jumped up against his chest, which forced Lance backward, onto the couch.

Then something else flashed: a blur of white that streaked across the hall. I whipped around, but it moved too fast. When I turned again, Ruby had taken the dog by the scruff of the neck while the animal howled in protest.

It all ended in less than a second. No one moved, except for the dog, which thrashed around wildly.

"Are you all right?" I moved to Lance and helped him rise from the couch.

"Think so. Ya gotta train that dog, Miss Ruby. He can't be jumping on people like that."

"I tol' ya . . . it ain't mine." She dragged the animal to the screen door, which she banged open with her foot, and then shooed it onto the front steps. "Anyway, he won't hurtcha." The door slammed shut behind the animal.

"Maybe we should go back to Hollis's room," I said. Anything to get away from the sound of the dog scratching its nails against the metal screen.

"You stay out here, Miss Ruby," Lance said. "We'll be a few minutes."

She didn't protest, and we walked through the kitchen and into the hall. One of the doors there stood open now: a cheap laminate panel shredded at the bottom. I cautiously stepped into what I assumed to be Hollis's room, since a poster of a half-naked character from *Mortal Kombat* hung on the wall and the air smelled like pot.

An unmade futon sat in the middle of the room. Gimme caps from rock groups—mostly Lynyrd Skynyrd and Kid Rock—hung from the plastic siding and a faded pillowcase covered the room's only window.

"I swear, something moved in here," I whispered to Lance. "Something shot across the hall when the dog came out."

I turned and stepped back into the hall, with Lance on my heels. After opening the door across from Hollis's room, I stepped into another bedroom. This one was lined with crucifixes and a lavender quilt covered the bed. Beyond the mattress stood another door, which rocked back and forth on its hinges.

"What do you know?" Lance said. "Hollis left through here."

"So she lied. Ruby must've seen him if she put the dog in his room." My voice sounded high and tight.

"Easy, there. You're not used to being lied to, are you? Don't worry. After a while it won't even faze you."

"I thought she was gonna help us." I glumly retreated into the hall. There was no sign of Ruby, but the dog continued to rake the screen door with its nails.

I returned to Hollis's dim room, where I spotted a light switch on the wall. I expected a burst of light when I switched it on, but a lavender glow eked out instead. Hollis must have switched out the lightbulb for a black light, and several things around the room glowed.

Orange and blue rocks lined a plywood shelf above the window. The trash can glowed pink from its spot under a makeshift desk built from two produce crates. A small pile of books lay on the desktop, along with a sketch pad.

I walked over to the desk and plucked up the first book. It was a graphic novel with two superheroes on the cover: Batman and Two-Face, who were engaged in an epic battle. The book below it was a manga comic with another topless girl on the cover, only this one held a smoking bazooka.

Curious now, I turned to the sketch pad. It reminded me of the Strathmore 400 I kept back at the studio, but any similarity ended there. Instead of wispy drawings of wedding veils, silk rosettes, and beaded headbands, Hollis had drawn superheroes missing various body parts. Batman had no arms and a river of blood ran down his legs. The next sketch wasn't any better: The topless girl from the poster was legless and snakes writhed in her hip sockets.

I shuddered and closed the sketch pad. *Interesting hobby.* I was about to give up on the desk when a final book caught my eye. It was black with a red triangle on its cover. I squinted at the title and brought it closer: *A Beginner's Guide to Voodoo and Hoodoo.*

I took it into the hall, where the light was better. The cover opened to a table of contents that listed spells alphabetically. There were spells for love, ones for money, and several for revenge. A whole chapter focused on spells meant to be said in front of a mirror. Hollis had drawn a star next to one that was titled *Kitchen Witchery—Using Everyday Items in Your Black Magick.* He'd scribbled what looked like "M.B." next to it.

I flipped to that chapter. First up was a list of ingredients, including everyday items like cayenne pepper and ginger, followed by some not-so-usual ones: pig's blood and taro roots, chicken feet and a slip of paper with the victim's name written on it. "Hey, Lance."

He'd knelt beside the trash can, which he'd overturned. "Yeah?"

"Look at this." I flashed him the book cover.

"What's it say? I can't see anything in this stupid light."

I walked back into Hollis's room with the book. "Looks like Hollis has been studying, all right. Just not sure it's something the school district knows about." I passed Lance the book and he quickly eyed the cover.

"Definitely creepy."

"The weird thing is that he marked a section on revenge," I said. "On spells you use to get back at people."

"Like Mellette Babineaux?"

"He wrote her initials next to it."

Lance frowned. "I'll need to bag it and tag it as evidence." He whipped an envelope from his back pocket and slipped the book into it.

"What if Hollis used a revenge spell on Mellette?" I asked. "Not only that, but what if he added something extra to make sure it worked? You told me the coroner's report was negative. Mellette wasn't bludgeoned or stabbed and she sure wasn't sick. That leaves poison."

"We still don't have a motive. Not really."

"He probably knew how Mellette treated his grandma." There was no mistaking the scowl on Ruby's face when Mellette ordered her to bring me some sweet tea. Even Mellette admitted Ruby probably had a voodoo doll back home with her likeness on it. "Maybe this was his way to get even with her."

At that moment, something moved in the doorway. It was Ruby, who'd balled up her fists and planted them against her hips. The cigarette was nowhere to be found. "Dat's wot ya tink? Ya tink ma Hollis done kilt Miss Babineaux? If dat's so, ya need ta leave."

Lance held up his hand. "And you need to back off. I told you to stay out front."

"But she ain't a cop. Why she be pawin' through my grandson's stuff?"

"She's helping me with this investigation," Lance said. "And your Hollis didn't do himself any favors by going to Sweetwater last night. Not while he's on probation."

Ruby's shoulders sagged. "But he's jus' a boy."

"You should have told us he was here," I said. "Then he could have spoken to us himself."

"She's right." Lance glanced at his watch. "If I was you, I'd bring your grandson to the police station this afternoon. Maybe he can explain himself."

Ruby wouldn't look at us as we passed her on our way to the kitchen. Once we walked through the dim living room, we stepped onto the porch. How wonderful to leave behind the smell of cigarettes, unwashed bedsheets, and fried hash browns. So wonderful that I forgot to worry about Jack, the mongrel.

Luckily, the dog seemed to have given up on us. I made it to Lance's car with no problem and moved into the passenger seat as Lance sat behind the steering wheel.

"Is it just me, or did that house give you the heebie-jeebies?" I asked.

"Nah, it's just you." Lance smiled as he revved the engine.

"She's a strange one." I glanced over my shoulder as we pulled away and saw Ruby's shrunken form behind the ripped screen. "I can't decide if I feel sorry for her or not."

"I don't. She should have been straight with us."

"True." I yawned loudly. "So where are we going? Back to the station?"

"We could." He glanced again at his watch. "But it's been awhile since I've had anything to eat. You up for some lunch?"

"I don't know. I'm trying to get the smell of that place out of my head. You'd think she'd wash the linens or something. But, yeah, now that you mention it, I could go for something to eat."

"So what about my mom's place? I know you said you ate there last night, but she's got a different lunch menu."

"Sure. Why not?" I leaned my head against the window, relieved to be sitting down again. Stands of cypress rolled by, their leaves blanched by the sun, and nothing moved in the sky above, which meant the egrets must have taken shelter from the midday heat.

"Shoot." I immediately straightened. "I should call my assistant at the shop. I've been gone for a while now."

I pulled out my cell and dialed the number, which rang twice before Beatrice picked up.

"Hi, Missy. Where are you?"

"Lance and I just left Miss Ruby's house. But we're thinking about getting some lunch. You okay over there?"

"Sure. It's been mostly quiet. Someone did call who got the number off our website. She wants to come in Friday."

"Great." Hallelujah! Some of our internet marketing was working. I'd spent a small fortune on a freelance designer and then hired an IT consultant who did something mystical called *search engine optimization*. "I'll look forward to it. No word from Jennalee, I hope."

"Nope. She's probably out spending Daddy's money. There was someone else who called, though. Someone from the management company here."

Just then Lance rounded a particularly steep curve and I lurched against the side panel. I shot him a look as we skidded back into our lane. "Did you say *management company*?"

"Yeah, the people who run the Factory. Remember that auction Jennalee was going on about? How they wanted to use the ground floor of her precious riverboat? Personally, I think it would've done her a world of good to share. But, whatever. Anyway, they called here."

"They want to have it at the store?" While I was proud of my studio—all 865 square feet of it—it was *not* designed to hold a public event.

"No, silly. They want to hold it in the atrium here. They're checking with all the shop owners to make sure it's okay."

Now, that made sense. Our landlord loved to host special events in the atrium, like wedding expos, flash sales, and monthly open houses. Anything to boost attendance and get people talking about our shops. "It's fine by me. You can say so if they call again."

"Will do. Have a nice lunch, and I'll see you when you get back."

"Just a second." Here Beatrice had been at the shop all morning, while I'd been gallivanting up, down, and sideways trying to find out more about Mellette's murder. "Why don't you leave the store yourself and grab some lunch?"

"Nah, I'm good. I'm saving room. Today they're giving out samples at Pink Cake Boxes."

I blinked. Was it really Tuesday afternoon already? I'd lost all track of time since Ambrose and I found Mellette's body on the dirty floor of the garden shed.

More than twenty-four hours had passed since then, and we still had no concrete leads.

I lowered the cell and leaned my head against the window again. After a few minutes, my eyelids grew heavy and I finally nodded off.

Chapter 12

"Rise and shine, sleepyhead. We're here." Lance's voice hovered somewhere over me.

Reluctantly, I pried my eyes open. We were in the parking lot of Miss Odilia's Southern Eatery, where everything looked the same, from the red brick walls faded pink to the purple flower boxes under the windowsills. The only difference was the empty parking lot.

Unlike the night before, when Ambrose and I could barely find a spot, only a few cars dotted the lot now. "Wow. You shoulda seen this place last night."

"Hope it was busier then."

"Definitely." I rubbed my stiff neck. "Could barely find a place to park."

I groped for the sunshade in front of me and flipped it open to check the mirror. Dark rings circled my eyes like two bruises, and a light sheen coated my skin. Thank goodness Ambrose was nowhere near me at the moment.

"Guess the crowd's lighter at lunchtime." Lance killed the ignition and swung open his car door.

I slapped the sunshade closed and stepped out of the car, onto the blacktop. Heat rose from the asphalt in waves, and I hotfooted it all the way to the front door. "Will your mom be here today?"

"I don't know," Lance said. "She could be at her other restaurant."

We walked under the kelly-green awning and approached the hostess, who recognized Lance immediately and motioned for us to follow her. Memories trickled back to me as we walked through the restaurant. Of Ambrose and me swaying across the floor after two bottles of white wine. The feel of his hand in mine as he led me through the tables. And then my surprise at seeing Hank Dupre and Ashley Cox together, just over there.

I thought I'd remembered everything until we passed by the awkward table in the alcove. It was where Charles had seated us. Maybe it was the exhaustion, but the hairs on the back of my neck began to bristle.

The chairs were gone now, replaced by rolled-up silverware, extra menus, and stacked water glasses. So why did the sight of it bother me so?

"You're back." A familiar voice sounded behind me.

I turned to see Charles, our waiter from the night before. "Hello. You know Lance, right?"

Since Lance was the detective at Morningside and Charles waited tables there, odds were good the two men knew each other.

He nodded. "Of course. 'Sup, Lieutenant?"

"A little of this and that. I'm working a case here in town. The Sweetwater case."

"Do you have any suspects yet?"

Lance shook his head. "No. I'm trying to eliminate some folks now. Don't have a whole lot to go on at this point."

While the two men talked, my mind returned to the night before. To a quiet conversation between Odilia and me, there in the awkward alcove.

"*Helllooo*. Whatcha thinking about?" Lance waved his hand in front of my face.

Charles had left and, in his place, he'd dropped two menus on the table.

"Nothing, really. Just how different everything seemed from when I was here with Ambrose last night. That's all."

"Um-hm." Lance pursed his lips as he pretended to study the menu.

"What? Okay, now you sound like your mother. Why can't people believe that he and I are just friends?"

"Friends don't look at each other like that."

"Like what? I look at him the same way I look at everyone else."

He struggled to keep a straight face. "You're probably the only one who doesn't see it. He can't seem to take his eyes off you. Guess you're the only one who hasn't figured it out."

"Whatever. By the way, why are you reading the menu? You should know your mama's food by heart."

"I do. Think I'm gonna go for the chicken and chutney today. Some people say it tastes like jelly, but there's a big difference."

The moment he mentioned the jelly, something clicked into place. *Of course.* Odilia had mentioned it somewhere near the end of our conversation.

We'd been talking about Mellette's murder and Sweetwater. Odilia wasn't surprised something terrible had happened there, given that people practiced witchcraft on the property. And not just any people . . . friends of Charles.

"You guys ready to order?"

Charles had returned to the table with a basket full of glazed rolls.

"Just a second." I pointed to a chair nearby. "Can we talk first?"

"I guess." He slid into the empty chair. "You're my only customers right now. 'Sup?"

"I want to talk to you about something I heard."

"Uh-oh. What've I done now?" Charles threw up his hands. He looked a bit disheveled again, as if he hadn't slept well. Maybe he was taking too many summer classes, though. "Whatever happened, I swear it wasn't me."

I squirmed in the chair. "Remember when Ambrose and I were here last night?"

"Of course. You guys had that weird table. Why?"

"Well, I had a chance to talk with Miss Odilia."

Lance suddenly looked up. Until now he'd been more interested in the menu than our conversation, but not after hearing his mother's name.

"I love working for her," Charles said. "She lets me pick my hours and the pay's decent. What about her?"

I paused before answering. I didn't want to put him on the defensive, but her comments had bothered me, so I picked my words carefully. "She told me about some of the friends you've made."

"Really?"

"She said you know those people who practice voodoo around here. Of course, I didn't believe her."

Something flickered behind his eyes. "I get it. You think I'm involved with all that voodoo stuff?"

"No. Maybe. I don't know." This wasn't coming out right. "I just think it's weird that you'd hang out with people like that."

"People like what?" Now it seemed like he was baiting me; daring me to say what was really on my mind.

"You know. People who cast spells and make potions and come up with curses. Weird stuff like that."

"Let me tell you something."

I hadn't been wrong. He definitely looked exhausted, and the anger only hardened his words more.

"Those people *are* my friends. Remember when my dad lost his fishing boat? We were dead broke after that."

How could I forget that? Charles had told me the story one day while we sat in the restaurant at Morningside, rolling up silverware all nice and tight. I'd asked him about his studies at LSU and why he still lived at home if he took classes almost two hours away, in Baton Rouge.

Everything came back to the day his father lost his shrimping boat. While Charles could cover the cost of tuition with his tips, he couldn't afford room and board too. So he moved back home, just in time to watch a sheriff arrive to repossess his dad's shrimping boat.

"No one wanted anything to do with us after that." His tone was ice cold. "Even our next-door neighbors turned their backs."

"That's terrible." I didn't know what else to say, and the memory seemed so fresh for him.

"The only people who talked to us lived along the river. They gave us bass and flathead; more than we could eat. They took my dad shrimping so he could get on his feet again. You just don't know them like I do."

I sucked in my breath. No wonder he'd befriended the women in batik skirts and tie-dyed headdresses, the ones who danced in the firelight. Turned out they not only made potions and cast spells and sewed gris-gris, but they also fed a family when no one else would.

Shame on me.

"On top of everything else," he said, "now they're losing their land. Some Realtors have already sicced the government on the old folks who live on the riverbank. They call the mobile homes an eyesore. Want to tear them down because the precious tourists might see it on their river cruises. I don't give a damn about the tourists. You don't kick old people out of their homes. That's just wrong."

He stalked away from our table without a backward glance.

"Wow. Guess he feels strongly about it." Lance watched him go.

"Now I feel terrible. I never should have said anything. Look what I started."

"You're okay. I can see why that stuff would surprise you."

"But he got so defensive." I'd never seen his jaw set so hard. "I don't think he's gonna talk to me again."

"You didn't mean any harm." Lance passed me a menu. "Here. Maybe some food will help take your mind off it."

"I don't even think I can eat."

"C'mon. Get yourself some chicken and maybe a glass of wine. My mom's cooking will help you feel better, since it sounds like you couldn't feel any worse."

We spent our lunchtime huddled over our plates, discussing Mellette's murder. By the time Charles brought us second cups of Community coffee, his face had relaxed again and I'd almost forgotten my earlier faux pas.

Much as I wanted to linger in the restaurant, both Lance and I had work to do. So we finished our coffees and left, with Lance waving to the hostess on our way out. Then he held open the front door for me, and I stepped into fresh air again. My eyes closed against the brightness, and that was when I almost ran smack-dab into someone else walking up the path.

"Lorda mercy!" My eyes flew open.

Odilia LaPorte swayed in front of me with a heavy Publix sack under each arm. I quickly reached for the nearest sack so she wouldn't topple over right then and there.

"Missy Du Bois." She gladly gave it to me. "Whatever are you doing here?"

"Having some lunch with Lance."

Her son stepped out from behind me and took the other grocery bag. "Hi, Mama."

"*Gah-lee*, that feels better." She shook out her wrists for a few seconds. "Do you mean to tell me you two have been here the whole time and I missed it?"

"Sure enough."

Her smile collapsed into a pout. "Gol-darn it! I coulda joined you."

"If it's any consolation," I said, "we just had the best meal ever. All thanks to your restaurant."

"You mean thanks to my chef. Think I've finally got that one trained."

"Where do you want the bags?" I asked.

"Over there." She motioned to the front door. "Put 'em right inside. I have to figure out where to put it all. Don't worry, nothing will melt. So, your food was good?"

"Of course." Lance's voice swelled with pride. "No wonder I weigh so much, Mama. I'm gonna blame you if I fail my next physical."

"Do I make you eat second helpings?" She tsked her way to the front door and waited for us to tuck the bags inside. "By the way, how's that murder case going?"

"It's going," Lance said. "Missy has been helping me with some leads."

"That's good. Hard to imagine something like that could happen right here in Bleu Bayou."

"You know it happens all over now." He turned to face me. "Mama here thinks criminals only hit big cities like New Orleans and Baton Rouge. I try to tell her it can happen anywhere."

"Do you know how she died?" Odilia scrunched up her nose. "Now don't tell me the gruesome parts. I haven't had my lunch yet."

"That's the thing," I said. "It looks like she may have been poisoned."

"Well, that's just as bad as anything else."

"But if they used poison, that means they put a lot of thought into it," I said. "It wasn't a random killing. Could be Mellette Babineaux even knew the person who did it."

At that moment, a car alarm began shrieking from somewhere in the parking lot. We all turned to watch the spectacle from the steps and to see whether someone would come running out of the restaurant. When no one did, we resumed our conversation, although we had to speak a little louder.

"It'll take six weeks for a toxicology report." I over-enunciated every syllable so she could hear me. "I'll bet you anything the coroner lists poison as the cause of death."

"Such a tragedy," she yelled. "And so close by."

Fortunately, the noise stopped as suddenly as it'd started. We all stared at the lot again, and my eyes swept along the wall nearest us, where the row of window boxes hung.

"I've been meaning to ask you something." The boxes held the most unusual arrangements of foxglove and calla lilies I'd ever seen. Someone had balanced the height of the callas against the depth of the foxglove, so the whole thing looked like a still life painted in watercolors. An underplanting of green-rimmed caladium only added to the beauty. "Who planted all the flowers around here? Was it you?"

"Me and my staff."

Lance eyed his mother. "Yep, my mom's a whiz with flowers. Just like she is with food."

"Go on." Odilia tried to wave away the compliment, but she wasn't fooling anyone. "It's easy to arrange 'em once you've got the right ones."

"That's the part I never can figure out." Without the blaring car alarm, I could speak in a normal voice again. "I never know what will grow here and what won't. Some of mine like the heat, but they can't take the frost."

"You know the gov'ment says we're in zone nine, right? Pick a zone-nine plant—maybe black-eyed Susan or wisteria—and you can't go wrong."

"That's where you lose me," I said. "It's hard for me to tell the difference between some weeds and plants down here. They all look alike if they have blooms."

Lance began to jiggle something in his pocket—probably his car keys—in an attempt to hurry us along. But I really wanted to know how anyone could keep their flowers so healthy in the August heat. I'd wasted buckets of money on plants since moving to Louisiana, so he could hold on for a minute or two. The investigation would still be there when we got back to the station.

And Odilia had warmed up to the topic. "I can loan you my *Farmer's Almanac*. It'll tell you everything you need to know about zone-nine plants, like these." She reached for a calla lily and tipped the bulb forward. "Now sometimes you have to be careful with these."

"With a calla lily?" I scrunched up my nose. "Why on earth?"

"People see a stalk like this, only greener, and straightaway they think it's a young calla. But let me tell you . . . you don't want to mess with anything that looks like this if you're out on the bayou."

Lance's jiggling grew louder and I shot him a look. "We're almost done, Lance. I don't get to talk to someone very often about flowers. Or at least someone who knows what they're talking about."

"Anyway, as I was saying—" Odilia gave him a stern look as well—"if you see something like this in the swamps, only greener, leave it alone. That's something called jack-in-the-pulpit. That stuff will burn your skin if you're not careful."

"Just by touching it?" The stalk she cupped in her hand looked so delicate.

"Um-hum. Sometimes. And it makes you sick if you get any in your mouth. The Indians knew that, way back when."

"Good to know. I'll be careful if I ever go out on the river again. Now, what's this one with the green edge . . . caladium, right?"

That pushed Lance right over the edge. "C'mon, Missy. You're killing me. I've gotta get back to work and you've gotta get back to that store of yours. Just call up Mom sometime and she'll teach you everything you want to know."

"All right." I tried to not sound as testy as I felt. "You never could hold onto your horses. I guess I'll have to talk to you later." I gave Odilia a quick peck on the cheek.

Lance sheepishly kissed her other cheek. "Sorry I have to run, but I've got lots of work to do."

We left Odilia there—after volunteering to unload her groceries one last time, though she refused—and headed for the parking lot. I paused when we arrived at Lance's car. "I almost forgot. I need to run when we get back to the station. Ambrose loaned me his cell phone and I still have it."

"Okay. Hop in."

I opened the passenger door and gingerly sat on the hot upholstery. Midafternoon sun glared through the windshield as we drove away.

Soon a line of smokestacks filled my view. They looked like shiny silver Q-tips, with puffs of steam stuck to the towers like wispy cotton balls. Before long we reached the police station and Lance pulled up next to Ringo, my VW.

"Thanks for lunch." I swung open the door. "We'll have to do it again."

"It was my mom's treat. She's told her staff not to charge me when I eat there."

"Then we'll definitely have to do it again. And don't forget to keep me in the loop if you hear anything new."

"I'll tell you what." He smiled at me, but his eyes were serious. "I'll do that if you promise not to run off by yourself and get in trouble."

"Deal." I stepped onto the warmed asphalt and slapped the side of his car, which felt gritty under my fingers. Sure enough, grime covered my fingertips when I pulled them away. *Great.* Maybe I should swing by the rent house first and wash up before I returned to work. It also wouldn't hurt for me to run a brush through my air before I saw Ambrose again.

I slid into Ringo and checked the glove compartment, just in case I had a stray Kleenex or Wet One. Instead, I found a Prismacolor art pencil, a folded sheet of sketch paper, which I always kept on hand, a few dressmaker pins, and a bottle of clear adhesive. There was no telling how long the Schick razor had been there.

Shrugging, I closed the compartment door and started the car. Now I had no choice but to return home and freshen up before heading back to the Factory. Ambrose had been without his cell phone this long, so what difference would it make?

Chapter 13

I steered onto the highway and pointed the car toward town. I had my choice of lanes, since few people traveled the road at three on a Tuesday afternoon. In fact, my only companion was a Martin oil tanker made entirely of stainless steel; every side reflected the scenery around it like a fish-eye lens. I watched in amusement as my car—or at least a squatter, flatter version of my car—pulled up behind it and spread out in the reflection.

When the off-ramp for Bleu Bayou appeared, I slowed to let the tanker pull away and drove onto the exit. After turning on the feeder road, I whizzed by the Factory first and then Dippin' Donuts—which looked empty now—and prepared to arrive home.

Before I reached it, though, I passed Sweetwater on my right. Crime-scene tape still stretched across the porch, the X of neon yellow harsh against the white columns. I couldn't resist the pull of the place and slowed to take a better look. While the bright tape still reminded me of a giant Band-Aid slapped on a wound, the strip that normally covered the front door was gone. Not only that, but the door stood open. Someone must have ducked under the tape to get inside and then forgot to close the door.

Shut my mouth and call me Shirley. Even though the sound of Lance warning me to not overstep my bounds echoed in my brain, what could I do? It wasn't like someone else would come along who cared about the old house. And the humidity would wreak havoc on the gorgeous floors and antique wall hangings. Or, heaven forbid, what if a curious squirrel took advantage of the situation and built a nest in the kitchen? The possibilities were endless; none of which I liked.

So I pulled off the road and parked at the lawn's edge. *Well, I'll just swaney!* Once again, the grille of Herbert Solomon's Rolls-Royce peeked out from behind the mansion, as shiny and obvious as the backside of that Martin tanker truck I'd followed on the freeway.

I threw open the car door, prepared to give him a piece of my mind and then some. First of all, the place was a crime scene. Although the perimeter was technically behind the house, the police had roped off the front area too. Second, what if Ashley showed up and found someone in his house? How could he explain his presence there without a Realtor?

My head swam by the time I reached the front door, and it had nothing to do with the heat and humidity.

Too bad I couldn't just throw open the door with a *bang* and make a dramatic entrance. Instead, I strode through the open doorway, into the foyer. The shades were drawn, which left everything shadowed and gray. I stood in the half-light and pondered my next move. Should I holler out his name? Tiptoe through the house until I found him? Or do both, and give him a chance to meet me halfway?

I began to rock on my heels. The hardwoods around me still shone like water on a bayou, and the mahogany panels engulfed me like a warm cigar box. As for the wall hanging . . .

I turned to take in the needlepoint tapestry of the herons, but it was gone. An outline remained—the wood inside the lines looked decades newer than the rest of the panel—but the tapestry had vanished.

Could it be? Mr. Solomon had mentioned something or other about the antiques here at Sweetwater. He'd used the term "godawful paneling," hadn't he? Not to mention "the fusty antiques."

It was too late for me to be nice anymore. "Mr. Solomon!" He should be drawn and quartered for messing with the beautiful interior of this house.

My voice echoed through the mansion. I waited a few seconds and then began to stride down the hall, toward the kitchen. Someone had switched on the pendant light over the sink, and the hammered copper shade bathed the room in a warm glow. I spied him there, hunched over the soapstone counter with yet another blueprint by his elbow.

"Mr. Solomon!"

He twisted and almost pitched headfirst into the sink. Praise the Lord, he managed to right himself at the last second.

"Don't do that, Miss DuBois." He spat out the words.

"I'm—I'm sorry." While my anger had propelled me this far, it stalled under his glare.

"That's a damn fine way for a person to enter a room."

"Look, I said I was sorry." I motioned behind me. "The front door was wide open."

"I was in a hurry." He waved the comment away. "Must've left it open by accident."

"What are you doing here?" Although the blueprint was obvious, I hoped he'd spare me the sarcasm this time.

"This and that. Hell of a time for this place to lose its real estate agent." He squinted at me. "I could ask you the same thing."

"I told you . . . the front door was open. I was worried about the heat and the animals."

He turned away, but instead of ignoring me like he'd done at the doughnut shop, he rolled up the blueprints and faced me again. "Think I'm all done here. I've seen what I need to see. And don't forget to close the door on your way out."

I reached for his arm when he turned. "Just a second."

He froze. Obviously no one had ever touched him like that.

"There was an antique out there," I said. "A tapestry." I relaxed my grip. "Do you know what happened to it?"

"How would I know?" He shook his shoulder, as if to erase my touch. "I never noticed it in the first place."

"But it took up the whole wall. I know you've been in the foyer, so you must have seen it."

"That's something my wife would notice, not me. I don't give a damn about the contents around here. Especially not some picture of birds. Now, if you'll excuse me—"

He started to move and I quickly blocked his path. "I thought you didn't notice the tapestry. But you knew there were birds on it. I didn't tell you that."

He glared at me again. "Look, Miss DuBois. I'm sure this is all very amusing for you. But if you're accusing me of something, I suggest you call your attorney first. No one calls me a liar and gets away with it."

I cringed. Surely he was bluffing . . . wasn't he? He would never involve an attorney. Would he? "I . . . I just thought—"

"I don't care what you thought. Unless you have proof, don't waste my time with your goddamn accusations. Good day, Miss DuBois."

He sidestepped me roughly, and the blueprint brushed against my shoulder. When he reached what I guessed to be the front door, his footsteps abruptly stopped.

"One other thing." His voice boomed in the quiet.

Come to think of it, I could hear him loud and clear from the kitchen, so he must've been able to hear me earlier. Not that he answered me . . . the weasel.

"Don't get your hopes up with this house," he yelled. "I put an offer in on it this morning. By tomorrow, I can take anything from it I want."

My knees felt weak. What did he mean, he put an offer in on the house? There was no way he could draw up a contract so quickly without a Realtor.

I leaned against the soapstone counter, while I frantically searched my memory. Last night, at Miss Odilia's restaurant, two men sat at a table. It was Hank Dupre and Ashley Cox, enjoying a leisurely meal together. They looked like old friends. Either that, or new business partners. Was that what this was about? Had Ashley hired Hank to sell his house? Not only that, had Hank already sold it to Mr. Solomon?

I gripped the counter's edge. There was only one way to find out: I could ask Beatrice. She'd know if her uncle was representing the property. Or, if she didn't know, she could call him and casually ask. Surely he'd tell his niece the truth.

To be honest, I had nothing but Mr. Solomon's word at this point. A man who obviously hated me and who obviously hated to be challenged.

I didn't bother to answer him. Instead, I straightened my shoulders and stalked out of the kitchen. By the time I reached the foyer, I'd decided to confront him, but it was too late. Much like the tapestry, Mr. Solomon had disappeared into thin air.

Once I'd returned to the rent house and changed, the afternoon sun had waned. Try as I might, I couldn't get the sound of Mr. Solomon's parting words out of my mind. If he did indeed own Sweetwater now, there wasn't a whole lot I—or anyone else, for that matter—could do about it. Except watch as a backhoe devastated the beautiful old oaks and a construction crew destroyed more than a century and a half of Southern history.

It was enough to make me cry into my gumbo. I worried a path all through my house as I gathered up comb, makeup, and clothes. I dressed quickly and then headed for the driveway, to Ringo.

Heaven only knew I'd rather not go back to work at this point. No, a nice hot bath and a deep dreamless sleep sounded much better. But all that would have to wait while I gave Ambrose his cell back and faced the music at Crowning Glory.

Soon enough, I drove the short distance to the parking lot at the Factory. Beatrice's pink pickup was in its usual spot toward the back, by Ambrose's Audi Quattro. I chose the same row and then made my way across the asphalt.

By now the usual parade of FedEx drivers, bridal entourages, and curious looky-loos had thinned. Only a few people walked through the lot, including a lanky mail carrier and a photographer with assorted camera lenses around her neck. Rings of sweat lined the armholes of her shirt, which meant she must've toiled outside today, bless her heart.

I followed them as far as the door to Ambrose's Allure Couture. Unlike my studio, which I'd decorated shabby chic by whitewashing the walls, slipcovering the chairs, and hanging sparkly crystals, Ambrose had taken the high road and gone for Parisian chic.

His studio featured fat plaster cherubs that floated from the ceiling. A row of gilded mirrors lined the walls, just like the hall at Versailles; rolling racks held puffy samples that billowed to the ground; and soft gray walls cocooned everything from the outside. The whole effect was ethereal, like a French boutique with a doorman and champagne on ice.

Behind this grand salon was another, entirely different, room. The stark white fitting room held a mirror, a rolling armchair, and a Singer CG590 machine for the seamstress. Ambrose would wheel the chair around during a fitting and watch a client walk back and forth, back and forth, in front of the three-sided mirror. That was how he knew which way a skirt moved as the bride walked.

Of course, magazine editors loved his attention to detail, and they regularly gushed about him in magazines like *Brides* and *Martha Stewart Weddings*. Even the foreign editors adored him, and his portfolio included featured stories in *Asiana Wedding*, *Sposabella*, and

Anhelo magazines. The National Bridal Market in Chicago awarded him its highest honor—the DEBI—which he promptly stowed away in a drawer and forgot about.

But before the Lucite trophy, or the elegant studio, or the exhaustive client list that stretched from New York to California, Ambrose had studied to be an architect. All that changed his sophomore year at Auburn, when the drama department needed sets for *A Midsummer Night's Dream* and his professor volunteered him.

It took him the whole second semester to construct a forest made of papier-mâché. When the costume designer flunked out, the same professor asked him to design costumes to match the elaborate sets. The professor awarded him a B for the sets, but the costumes landed him on the dean's list.

The rest, as they say, is history. Of course, Bo's detractors have always suggested that real men don't design wedding gowns. *What a crock.* I wish they could see his year-end statements now that his gowns command ten thousand dollars a pop.

Luckily, I saw him right away when I walked into his studio. He was rearranging sample dresses on one of the rolling racks.

"Hey, Ambrose." Unlike me, Bo looked fine, despite our late night.

The traitor.

"Missy!" He glanced up. "I've been missing my phone all day. Can I have it back?"

"Of course. I didn't mean to borrow it for so long. But then one thing led to another . . ."

"I'll bet. Let me guess: You finally had lunch with that cop you know."

"Yep." I reached into my pocket and tossed him the phone. "We went back to Miss Odilia's place. That's a whole story in itself."

He shot me a funny look. "But that's where we ate dinner last night."

"It's his mom's place, remember? I didn't want to tell him no."

"Guess I understand that. How was your meal?" Ambrose looked at the rack again and rifled through it until he found a certain mermaid gown, which he moved forward.

"Good, but that's not all that happened." I waited for him to rearrange the rack some more, hoping it would distract him from what

I was about to say. "By the way, I kinda went back to Sweetwater today."

No such luck. "Now, why would you do that?" His hand stalled in midair. "You promised me you wouldn't go back there on your own."

"I never said that." Which was true enough, but it didn't seem to help matters any. "I told you I was going to meet up with Lance, but I never said anything about Sweetwater."

"You should have told me first."

"I didn't have a choice. The front door was wide open. What could I do? Trust me, you have no idea where I've been today."

"And I'm not sure I want to know. I think it's time for you to let the police handle this. Past time, actually."

There, he'd said it. What I knew Ambrose had been thinking all along. He wanted me to leave the investigating to Lance and go on my merry way. While he was probably right, something about his tone of voice made me dig in my heels. "For your information, the door was wide open. Anyone—or anything—could have wandered into that house out of the clear blue. Mellette isn't around to protect it anymore, and someone's gotta do it."

"Why?"

His curt response silenced me. *Why, indeed?* Several reasons floated through my head, but when I tried to snatch one, I got lost in Ambrose's beautiful sky-blue eyes all over again. More of a Tiffany blue, actually—

"Well?"

I glanced away. "We already went over this. Mellette was my sorority sister. She's dead now and the police don't have any leads. The first twenty-four hours are critical after a murder. If you haven't noticed, we're past that now."

"Of course I noticed." He reached over the clothing rack. "Look at me." He gently lifted my head with his hand.

Too bad a dozen yards of satin and silk stood between us, because I would've liked to inhale his Armani cologne at the same time.

"I don't want you going over there anymore. You could get in trouble."

Damn him and those eyes. Especially when they looked soft, like now, which meant he wasn't mad anymore . . . he was worried. "Why, Ambrose Jackson. I do think you're concerned for my welfare."

"Of course I'm worried about you. We share a house together."

"So that's it." I stepped back so his hand would fall away. "You only want me to stay safe because we're roommates. Argh! I should've known as much."

"No, no. Of course not. I'm kidding."

Now was probably not the right time or the right place to speak my mind, but I couldn't help myself. Maybe because I hadn't slept in forever and Odilia's words kept running through my mind. "We've been friends for a long time now, Bo. I've been patient, but just how long can a girl wait?"

"You've been great. Look—"

Before he could say more, the mail carrier I'd seen outside walked into the studio with a package under her arm.

"I've gotta go." I moved away from the rack before he could stop me.

"Don't. Please don't go."

But I'd dug in my heels so deep that even his gentle prodding couldn't move me. "Look, I've been away from my studio for hours. It's not fair to Beatrice. See you later."

I sped away, knowing the mail carrier would probably block Ambrose if he tried to follow me. If he was so concerned about my gosh-darn welfare, he should gin up and say something, like Odilia had mentioned. He could ask me out on a real, honest-to-goodness date. But every time I tried to bring the subject up to him, he said something funny and we got off track again. I could never seem to bring us back 'round again once that happened.

I studied the floor as I walked. Travertine tile gave way to a rush welcome mat and then pavement as I stepped outside. Our two studios shared a wall, so the window for mine appeared right away. Through it I could see Beatrice standing by the counter, a stack of mail in her hand.

She glanced up when I walked into Crowning Glory. "I haven't seen you in hours. Thought you might've gone home to catch up on your sleep."

"Nah, I've got too much going on today." I flopped onto a stool beside her. "Anything new here?"

"Let's see." She peeked at a schedule taped next to the cash register. "MaryLouise Scarborough wants to come in first thing tomorrow morning for her fitting, not Thursday. I said that was fine. And that gal who called off the internet? She wants to come in tomorrow now too. Looks like we're gonna have a busy day."

"As long as it's not Jennalee Prudhomme, I don't mind."

Beatrice cocked an eyebrow. "What's wrong? You look kinda down."

"I'm just tired. That's all. I've driven all over Louisiana today. But at least I had a nice lunch with Lance LaPorte. He's the one who called here this morning."

"That's right. He said something about getting a search warrant. What was *that* all about?"

"Remember the voodoo ceremony I told you about? Hollis Oubre was there, of all people. Lance wanted to look around his grandma's mobile home, and I said I'd go with him."

Beatrice pursed her lips. "Hollis Oubre, huh? Now there's a strange one."

"What do you mean?"

"I heard he got kicked out of high school. Something about putting a curse on another kid. Creepy stuff like that."

"That makes sense. He's supposed to be homeschooled now. But we didn't find any textbooks in his room. We *did* find a book about voodoo. He'd even written an M and a B next to one chapter . . . like in *Mellette Babineaux*."

She shrugged. "That could mean anything. A lot of people use it for 'maybe' when they're texting, and people who write on message boards use it too." She began to leaf through the pile of mail. "Guess I should probably handle the bills first. And the bank statements."

Since Beatrice handled the books for the studio—in addition to helping with customers and whatnot—I was more than happy to let her have them.

"At least give me the letters on the bottom. Those don't look like statements."

She split the pile in two and gave me half. My mail was mostly ads for local stores and car dealerships, but one oversized postcard stood out. It was a plain card with ink-jet printing. The front showed a wall hanging that reminded me of the tapestry back at Sweetwater. Even though Sweetwater's had herons on it and not peacocks, like this one, both were the same size and shape.

"Well, that's weird." I held up the card. "They had a tapestry like this one at Sweetwater. A different pattern, but the same size and everything."

"Lemme see that."

I handed her the card, which she studied for several seconds.

"It's an ad from the auction house," she finally said. "For a preview party tomorrow night. That's the place that usually works on the *Dixie Queen*." She turned the card over. "Gee, even I could afford this one."

I leaned over her shoulder. The text said something about bidding starting at fifty dollars, which seemed ridiculously cheap, since the tapestry was so big and in such good condition. "Wonder if they always sell their stuff so cheap?"

"I doubt it. The furniture and other stuff probably goes for a whole lot more. My uncle said auction places try to sell textiles first because they don't bring much. That's why rugs aren't a good investment, no matter what anyone tells you."

So much for the Oriental rugs I'd seen advertised in fancy decorator magazines. Sad to think people would only get pennies on the dollar if they ever sold them. "That's gotta suck if you're the seller."

"Yeah, it does. My uncle said people have to be desperate to sell off their textiles."

My eyes widened. "Dag-gum-it!"

"What?"

A memory flickered by. Herbert Solomon and I had stood in the kitchen at Sweetwater, by the soapstone counter. He'd been shocked by my suggestion that he might have taken the tapestry off of the wall. So shocked he threatened to sic an attorney on me if I ever said it again. "I kinda accused Herbert Solomon of taking something like this from Sweetwater."

"Tell me you didn't." Beatrice tried to be serious, but a smile played on her lips. "I can't believe you said that."

"What am I gonna do? I honestly thought he took it. He was the only one in the house this morning and the wall was blank. I saw a big ol' tapestry there yesterday and today—poof—it's gone."

"You do know that Herbert Solomon is one of the richest men in Louisiana, right? He must've died when you said it."

"He did. He threatened to call his attorney. I thought he was bluffing, but you never know."

She finally sobered up. "Okay, so you made a mistake. Maybe he'll forget about it the next time he sees you."

"Yeah, right. He doesn't seem the type to forget anything."

"I don't know what to tell you. But I doubt a billionaire would steal something that sells for less than a hundred dollars." She held the card up to the light. "Anyway, I wouldn't mind going to this thing on Wednesday and seeing what else they have. Wanna go with me?"

"Huh? Yeah, sure." One last memory pinballed around my skull, refusing to be ignored. It was Herbert Solomon again, only this time he stood by the front door and yelled at me. Told me he'd purchased Sweetwater and he could take anything from it he wanted, starting tomorrow. "He said something else. Something shocking."

"Like what?"

"He told me he bought Sweetwater. Said it belongs to him now."

"Really?"

"Sure did. But I can't believe it, since the house doesn't even have a real estate agent. Who would write up the contract?"

"Maybe he got someone else."

"Bingo. And I think I know who it is. I saw your uncle last night at dinner. He was there with one of the guys who own Sweetwater. They looked like friends."

"Friends? That doesn't sound right. The owners are young and they don't even live here anymore. Don't think my uncle would be friends with one of 'em."

"That's what I thought. Is there any way you can find out? Maybe call your uncle and ask if he's representing the property?"

"I guess so. But it's really none of my business."

"That's okay." I slid off the stool. "I'm making it your business. It's time for me to go home, or else I'm gonna fall asleep right here."

She set the postcard aside. "No problem. I'll lock up. Hope you get some sleep tonight."

"Me too." I left the studio and walked to the parking lot. Most of the cars were gone now, except for Ringo and a lonely-looking U.S. Post Office van. I'd have to remember to thank my letter carrier later for running interference for me in Ambrose's studio.

Chapter 14

I drove away from the Factory in a fog. While I'd planned to make a nice, hot dinner when I got home—and maybe even pair it with a glass of Merlot—that all changed the minute I walked through the door. Instead, I made a beeline for my bedroom and flopped onto the mattress fully clothed. I didn't wake up until a noise sounded on the other side of the door.

"Missy?"

I moaned and rolled over. It was Ambrose, of course, calling to me from the hallway. "Hmmm. Yeah. I'm in here."

"Can we talk?"

I ran my hand across my eyes. How long had I been asleep? Apparently long enough for Ringo's key to make a perfect imprint on my right palm. "I guess so."

The door swept open. Ambrose lingered in the doorway with his hands in his pockets, instead of barreling into my room like he usually did. "I just wanted to tell you I'm sorry."

He looked sorry; his gaze studied the floor instead of my face. But I wasn't ready to give him a pass. He'd hurt my feelings, and I wasn't going to pretend that he hadn't. "For what?"

"You know . . . for stuff."

He looked miserable, or about as miserable as a house cat in a rainstorm, as my grandpa said. While I wasn't one who normally enjoyed watching other people suffer, it wouldn't hurt for him to twist in the wind a bit. "What kind of stuff?"

"Can I just come in and sit down?"

"Suit yourself."

He walked into the room and awkwardly perched on a corner of the bed. Although I must have looked a fright, he didn't seem to notice, because he reached for my right hand and gently rubbed at the key's imprint.

"I know you're mad at me," he said. "And I think I know why. I haven't been very honest with you."

"Do tell."

"It's true. And I'm not gonna lie to you now and say I have everything figured out. But you've been patient while I got over, you know . . ."

There was no need for him to finish. We both knew what he was talking about. Ambrose had married his first love, a pretty catalogue model he'd met in college. She died not more than two years later, which nearly killed *him*.

"You know, it's okay if you want to talk about it with me," I said. "I don't mind."

"I know you don't. But I feel like I've been taking advantage of you all this time."

I started to protest, but he brought his other hand to my lips.

"Let me finish. I've been taking advantage of your patience. I do want to be more than friends with you."

It was hard to decide which of the two I enjoyed more: the feel of his hand on my lips or the sound of his precious words.

"In fact, I've been thinking about it all night. Missy DuBois . . . will you go out with me?"

I cracked an enormous grin. So much for being coy. "Why, yes. I'd be honored to go out with you."

"How about Friday night? And I'll even treat you to breakfast now. Sort of like a trial run. I happen to know a place around the corner that makes the best beignets."

Apparently I'd been asleep for twelve hours and never once stirred. "That sounds good to me. Give me half an hour to shower and change. By the way, the gentleman usually pays."

He smiled back at me. "Of course. You're worth it."

As he bounded out of the room, so different from the way he'd entered it, I flopped back on my mattress and bit into my pillow so I wouldn't scream. Maybe things were turning around, after all.

Thirty minutes later I entered the kitchen wearing another of my favorite Lilly Pulitzer shifts. This one's print was a tad splashy, but I wanted to look as good as I felt. I walked up behind Ambrose and peered over his shoulder at the business section of the *Times-Picayune*. "Ready to go?"

He turned around and smiled. "Don't you look bright this morning."

When he rose, he offered me his arm. Somehow we maneuvered through the tiny cottage side by side until we emerged into bright sunshine. The Audi waited for us near the listing garden gate.

He held open my door and I climbed into the passenger seat. Neither of us said much as we began the drive to Dippin' Donuts, which was fine by me. After a few minutes, we passed a Shell oil tanker and then a cargo van for UniFirst uniforms. Before long, Ambrose made a hard right and we arrived at the bakery's parking lot.

Cars buzzed in and out of the parking lot. Beatrice's pink Ford was parked in the second row, next to a blue Chevy Nova. I didn't have time to wonder about Ruby Oubre, though, because Ambrose immediately swerved the car into a parking space and yanked the keys from its ignition.

"Let's go. I'm famished." He jumped out of the car and hustled over to my side.

Once I took his hand and stepped onto the asphalt, we practically ran to the plate-glass door, which he threw open. Sure enough, Beatrice stood by the doughnut case, with Ruby behind her, when I entered.

Beatrice waved to me. "Hey, you look a thousand times better."

"Gee, thanks." I joined her by the case. "Now there's a backhanded compliment if ever I've heard one."

"You know what I mean." She motioned to Grady, who stood behind the case. "I was just about to order a beignet."

He waved. "Hi, Missy. What—"

Ambrose walked through the door just then and joined us.

"Did Missy tell you guys she slept twelve hours last night?" Ambrose said. "Thought I was gonna have to pry her out of her bed with a crowbar."

I jabbed him in the ribs with my elbow. "You did not. And yesterday was the longest day of my life. I was a zombie . . . I'm amazed I got anything done."

"You're kidding, right?" Beatrice rolled her eyes. "You two should have seen her go at it in the studio. This horrible bride came in and threw a hissy fit." Beatrice pouted like Jennalee had done. "Anyway, most people would have told that girl where to go. But not Missy. She whipped up a new design in no time flat and saved the day. Course, I still wanted to punch Bridezilla."

"Why doesn't that surprise me?" Ambrose's voice was thick with pride. "Just when you think she can't top herself, she goes and does it."

"Congrats." Grady's eyes darted over our heads. "Look, I hate to do this, guys, but I've gotta get back to work. What can I get you?"

I started to place my order, but then I remembered something. Ruby had been standing behind us the whole time, patiently waiting while we chitchatted about this, that, and the other thing. I swiveled around. "Do you want to go ahead of us?"

Today she wore a bright-purple LSU T-shirt with a matching sun visor. She smelled like cigarette smoke, even so early in the day. "Nah, go on. Don't take dat long ta order."

I turned around again and asked for two raspberry beignets and a large coffee. Once Ambrose had placed his order and then paid for our food, I pulled him aside. "Listen, I want to talk to Ruby for a few minutes. Do you mind?"

"Not at all. I'll find us a table in the back. But don't take too long or I may have to start in on your food."

"Don't you dare!" I would've pinched him in the arm for good measure, but the hot coffee in his hand swayed me. "I'll be just a second. Try to behave yourself for that long."

He wandered away, trailing the sugary smell of fresh beignets behind him, and I turned to face Ruby. "Are you eating alone?"

"Nah. Takin' dem home. I gots lotsa time for breakfast now."

"That's right. Guess you're not working at Sweetwater anymore."

She blew out a puff of air. "*Pfffttt.* Deys don' need me now. Da police have dat place all roped off. Can't touch it 'til dey done."

"Well, it *is* a crime scene. Say, I noticed something yesterday. Something strange." I waited for Grady to pass her some doughnuts from the case. "I was at the house. Just Herbert Solomon and me."

Her eyes narrowed. "Whatcha two be doin' dere? Ain't nobody supposed to be dere. How'd ya get in?"

"That's the thing. The front door was wide open. I think Mr. Solomon forgot to close it. Remember that big tapestry in the front hall? The one with birds on it? I always thought it looked like a scene from the Gulf of Mexico."

"Yeah, I know da one. Why?" She handed Grady a couple of dollars in exchange for the doughnuts.

"It's not there anymore."

"Dey stole it? I knew dose boys was trouble."

I assumed she was talking about the Cox brothers. "But they own the house. Why would they take anything from their own house?"

"Hard ta say. But dose boys be like Cain and Abel. One wants wot da other one has. Dey don' git along."

I began to chew my lower lip. "I've only met one of them. And they know they're going to inherit the money once the house sells, so why would they take anything? Plus, Ashley Cox already told me they sold a lot of the good stuff when their mom died and they replaced it with fakes."

"Some a' dat stuff ya can't fake." Ruby shook her head. "Maps and ol' letters, pictures even. Lotsa pictures. Dat's why da museums wanta buy it. Collectors too. So many people come 'round to look at it."

My breath stalled. I had no idea the property was so popular. I'd assumed everyone would be turned off by its peeling paint and small rooms, or that was what I'd hoped would happen. Somehow I still nursed visions of Ambrose and me on the front porch with the sun lightening the columns all around us, no matter what anyone said.

Ruby cocked her head. "Don'tcha know? Da Confederates used Sweetwater durin' da war. Ta hide stuff dere."

"Then how did it survive the war?" I'd seen pictures of the Great River Road during the Civil War days, back in the museum at Morningside. Blurry photographs with smoky sugarcane fields and scorched, black earth where elegant plantations once stood.

Thankfully, not all plantations suffered the same fate, I'd learned. One Union officer told his men to hold their fire when he came upon Morningside and realized he'd been to a dance there the year before. Another plantation earned a pass because its owners had sons in both the Union and Confederate armies.

"Ya heard about da Freemasons?"

"Sure. They're the ones with a square and compass on their signs."

"Da owner of Sweetwater was a Freemason. So when da troops come, he gives 'em da secret sign an'—*et voilà*—turns out da general was one too."

"Wow. Mellette never told me that."

"Yep. No one done touch it after dat. So deys hid papers an' such.

Why do ya tink I worked dere fo' so long? Dat place be special ta lotsa folks."

"Does everyone else know about this?"

"Not sure. Look, I gots to go. Hollis will be waitin' on his food. Check out da history books. Deys chock fulla stories."

She walked past me and disappeared through the exit. She seemed to know a lot about the history around here, while I was learning such interesting tidbits, one by one.

Chapter 15

I waited for Ruby to leave before searching for Ambrose. He was sitting in a booth toward the back of the doughnut shop, with the still-unopened bag of beignets on the table. Bless his ever-lovin' heart.

Before I could signal to him, someone grabbed my elbow. I turned to find Lance, who was wearing a short-sleeved police shirt today, behind me. He must've arrived while I was talking to Ruby.

"There you are," he said. "I tried calling your studio, but no one answered."

"My assistant just left and I'm here with Ambrose. He's buying me breakfast this morning. By the way, you can wipe that grin off your face."

"Who, me?"

He did his best to look innocent, although I wasn't fooled. "I know what's running through that head of yours right now, so you can just knock it off."

"Okay." He dropped the grin. "Here's the thing: I got a fingerprint report back on the Sweetwater murder."

"So soon?"

"Yeah. Normally it takes a week, but it's a slow time for them. I'd rather not get into it right here. Why don't we take a table or something?"

"Let me talk to Ambrose first. He's waiting for me to join him."

I walked back to Ambrose but, instead of sitting down, I reached into the bag and plucked out a beignet. "Would you please take one? I ran into Lance up there and he wants to show me a report on Mellette's murder. I'd like to hear about it. Do you mind?"

"Lance, huh?" He accepted the beignet and took a big bite from its end.

"He said something about getting the fingerprint analysis back early."

It took Ambrose a moment to finish chewing. "No, I don't mind. But I know you don't like cold beignets."

Which was true enough. Every time I ate one, it reminded me of a lump of paste. Thankfully, Grady kept a microwave by the Bunn coffee machine, which I knew he'd let me use.

"It's okay," I said. "I can pop it in the microwave later. I promise I won't be more than five minutes."

"Toss me a section of that newspaper first." Ambrose pointed a powdery finger at the trash can, where someone had thrown a disheveled copy of the *Times-Picayune* on top. "And I'll be fine."

I walked to the trash can and grabbed the paper. Once I'd handed it to Ambrose, I headed for a long counter Grady had nailed into the eastern wall of the shop. Lance sat on a stool there, with a powder-blue folder on the counter in front of him.

"No doughnuts for you today?" I slid onto a stool next to him.

"Nah. I'll have something later. Hope Ambrose didn't mind you leaving him like that."

"He's reading the newspaper. And the beignets can wait. So, what did they find at Sweetwater?"

"I'll give you the Cliffs Notes version, since the report's pretty long. I want you to tell me if anything rings a bell, since you were at the house before the investigator dusted for prints."

"Sure thing." It was nice to be able to discuss a case with Lance without him telling me it was none of my business.

"Bottom line is there's good news and bad news." He picked up the folder. "The good news is they got to the body within two hours. You can't pull prints off skin that's been left alone for longer than that."

"That means the killer must have come to Sweetwater right after Ambrose and I left."

Lance nodded. "You got it. They pulled some latent prints, which are the ones you can't see by using powder."

"Great. What'd they find?"

"There's the bad news. It's hard to pull a print from a body since you're talking about skin-to-skin contact. They got prints, all right, but the oils got all mixed up, so none of them are clear."

"Which means they couldn't read them? What about her business suit?"

"More bad news. Her jacket was a cotton blend—rough and raw. The more porous the clothes, the harder it is to pull off clean prints."

"You're telling me they didn't get anything?"

"They found prints, all right, but most of them were the victim's. First thing they do is powder the entrance and exit of a crime scene. Since the shed only had one entrance, it made the job a whole lot easier. Miss Babineaux's prints were all over that."

I gasped. "But what about Ambrose's and mine? We went into the shed through that door too."

"We found some for Ambrose, all right. We already had his prints on file because of the murder at Morningside. They didn't find any of yours."

"He must've opened the door for me, like he always does." I could picture Ambrose and me approaching the listing door of the cottage. It was a Dutch door, like something the seven dwarfs might've used. The top half was open, but the bottom half wasn't. I'd smelled menthol cigarettes the moment I'd walked through it. "I'm sure that's what happened."

"We guessed that."

"But the door was wood and the knob was brass, I think. Those aren't porous," I said. "They should've found the criminal's prints too."

"Bingo," he said. "I like the way you think. It should've been covered with prints. But there weren't any others. Nada."

"Which would mean the guy—or the girl—must've worn gloves."

"Yep. Clean as a whistle. It's the only way that door would come up clean."

"Then it was premeditated, all the way. Otherwise the criminal wouldn't have brought gloves. Which points back to my theory about poisoning."

"I agree with you there. The killer didn't leave anything behind. No hairs, no fibers, no nothing. But we don't know the poison and we won't 'til we get the tox report back probably for several weeks."

"What if—"

At that moment, a streak of purple and white rushed up to us.

"—goodness gracious," I said.

Ruby skidded to a stop in front of us, her face flushed to high heavens and her breathing labored. "Ma boy's done gone."

"Whoa . . . hold on there," Lance said. "What are you talking about, Miss Oubre?"

"He done left da house wit da door open. Cain't find my dog, neither. He ain't never done dat before. Never."

She couldn't catch her breath, so I slid off the stool and offered it to her. "You'd better sit down, Miss Ruby. You look kinda pale."

She gratefully took the seat. "I done got back in ma car. Saw yer cruiser in da parkin' lot here." She spoke to Lance, but her eyes flittered from his face to mine. "Ya gots ta help me."

"Maybe he went for a walk," I said.

"Dat boy knows better den ta leave dat door open. He ain't dere. He ain't nowhere."

I glanced at Lance. "Maybe he went to find his friends. The ones we saw him with on Monday night."

"Ya tink he done run off ta Mother Belle? Deys some bad people dere. He could be in trouble den."

"You're getting ahead of yourself," Lance said. "Did you try calling his cell?"

"Four times. Maybe five. Dat boy always take my call. He be in trouble. I can feel it."

She was becoming more and more agitated, her legs twisting and untwisting. "Wot am I gonna do?"

"Guess we should go look for him," I said. "Do you have any idea where he could've gone?"

She finally stopped moving. "He like da comic book store. Dat's by da liquor store. Maybe dat's where he be. Gah-lee, dat boy done scare me half ta death."

"I'll take you there, Miss Ruby." Lance eyed me. "You go back to Ambrose and eat your breakfast. I'll let you know what we find out."

"Okay. And please call me if they find anything else in the shed." Luckily, Miss Ruby's complexion had evened out by now and her breathing seemed steady. I began to walk away from the counter, relieved to hand over the reins to Lance, when I remembered something and glanced back. "Don't worry about your dog, Miss Ruby. I'm sure he'll come back."

Her eyes looked doubtful. "Tank ya."

Although I had no way of knowing whether the mutt would actually return, it couldn't hurt to comfort Ruby in her time of need. She obviously had a soft spot for Jack, whereas I'd written him off as a menace.

I made my way to the back of the doughnut store. Hallelujah, the bag of beignets still sat on the table, although it looked a little thinner now. "Whew." I plopped beside him on the bench. "Glad I escaped that bullet. Miss Ruby can't find her grandson and Lance is gonna help her. The last thing I need to do is go back to the bayou."

"It wasn't that bad, was it?"

"Near enough." A feathering of powdered sugar dusted Ambrose's bottom lip. While I longed to kiss it away, I reached over and brushed it off with my hand. "I'd much rather be here with you. Someone has to keep you decent."

"Whatever you say. Hey, I've been thinking about all the places we could go on our date Friday night. I think you'd like that restaurant called Commander's Palace in New Orleans. You up for that?"

"Commander's Palace?" But that was an hour away. Which meant our date could easily stretch into the wee hours—or, heaven help me—overnight. That was, if we both played our cards right.

Chapter 16

A fter asking Grady to warm my breakfast, I finished eating and Ambrose drove us back to our place, where I retrieved Ringo and then headed back to the Factory for what I knew would be a busy day.

Sure enough, by the time I arrived at Crowning Glory, Beatrice had her hands full with our first bride of the day.

MaryLouise Scarborough was a former champion baton twirler—a fact she'd managed to work into our very first telephone conversation, bless her heart—and she still had the posture to prove it. The girl sat ramrod-straight in one of the armchairs with her feet delicately crossed at the ankles.

I could tell Beatrice had done her best to occupy her, since a slew of bridal magazines sprawled across the floor, but they both looked relieved to see me when I walked in.

"You're here!" Beatrice waved me over.

"Yep. Right as rain now I have some food in me. You must be MaryLouise." I walked to the armchair with my hand outstretched.

When the girl rose, I nearly fell over backward. No wonder she was a champion twirler; she nearly touched the clouds. My guess was six foot five, at least.

"Nice to meet you," she said.

Not surprisingly, her grip was nice and strong. "Likewise."

"I've heard so much about your studio. You get great reviews on the internet."

"That so? Must be my friends and family." I winked and led her over to the mirror. "Let's try on different styles so I can get an idea of what you're looking for."

She eyed a tiny fascinator that perched on a nearby stand. While most people expect me to dress a tall girl in a close-fitting hat—like a fascinator, which wouldn't add any more height to her frame—I knew better.

I bypassed the fascinator for another display. One that held an ivory riding crop, a pair of lace gloves, and a silk ascot. A white satin top hat ringed with French netting completed the display. It was one of my favorites, and I knew it'd be perfect for my bride.

I plucked it up and headed back to the mirror. Before I could place it on MaryLouise's head, though, she reeled away from me.

"Heavens, no. I could never wear that." Her eyes were twice their normal size. "It'd make me look like a giant. Don't you have anything nice and small?"

"That's the point. You have to trust me on this."

I gently took her shoulders and turned her away from the mirror. Then I placed the top hat on her head and spun her around until she faced the glass once more.

"See?" The proportions worked perfectly. An extra four inches balanced out her limbs and torso and drew attention to her face. "Tall people usually reach for small hats, but that's a big mistake. Large frames need large hats. The bigger, the better. Otherwise it looks like your head is out of proportion with the rest of your body."

"I get it." MaryLouise tilted her chin and smiled, while she studied her reflection.

"That one's pretty on you." Beatrice had walked up behind us. "And since you're getting married outside, you can wear something a little more casual."

I stepped away from the women and reached for the fascinator I'd seen earlier. "Let's try an experiment." I walked back to the mirror with the delicate hat, which had a base no bigger than a teacup saucer. I handed it to MaryLouise, who balanced it on her head and immediately laughed.

"See what I mean?" I asked.

"Okay. You're right." She couldn't wait to take off the hat. "No small hats for me."

"Let's try on some more."

I walked her through the various styles—all oversized this time—I'd put on display. Everything from wide-brimmed picture hats to a straw derby with a velvet hatband and a lampshade hat with a sheer brim. Each time, though, we returned to the top hat with its gauzy netting and dusting of seed pearls.

"Why don't you sleep on it, before you order this one," I said. "If you still want it in the morning, I'll create a custom piece based on this one."

She nodded enthusiastically. "Gotcha. And promise me you won't show that top hat to anyone else in the meantime!"

"We'll see." I returned the hat to its display, while smoothly deflecting her request. Part of my job involved diplomatically sidestepping demands like that one. Of course I'd let another girl try on the top hat if it struck her fancy. For some reason, every client wanted her hat to be the most unique creation that had ever walked down a wedding aisle. Which was possible, up to a point. I could embellish the heck out of a hat, but I couldn't change its basic form. Not that my brides wanted to hear that.

"See you tomorrow!" MaryLouise whisked open the front door and practically skipped out of the studio.

I turned to Beatrice the moment the door closed behind her. "Now that was one tall drink of water. Bet she was a featured twirler in college."

"Probably." Beatrice had returned to the counter and picked up our pile of mail again. She leafed through the pile until she found the postcard we'd discussed earlier. The one with a tapestry on its front that should've cost a whole lot more. "And I wasn't kidding when I said I wanted to go to this thing tonight. It starts at six in the atrium. Will you be my date?"

"Sure, I'll go with you. I've never been to an auction preview."

We still had a full day's work ahead of us, though, and heaven only knew how many more dramas we'd face between now and then.

The rest of the day whizzed by. One of my favorite clients, who was a physician who'd met her police-officer fiancé in the emergency room, came in for her first fitting. She'd chosen a theatrical boater with oodles of tulle, so I first measured her head and traced the dimensions onto a piece of insulation foam, which would give me a template later on.

After she left, I split my time between two other projects. Normally, I stopped taking custom orders at around four pieces or so, or else everything would start to get muddled in my brain and then I'd only get frustrated.

Time sped by. When I finally glanced up from my sketch pad,

wisps of hair fluttering around my face, it was already six, according to my cell phone. I tossed down the Prismacolor pencil and stretched, realizing—once again—I'd forgotten to eat lunch.

Lately I'd gotten into the bad habit of skipping meals. Thank goodness Beatrice usually made it her business to watch out for me, and she often snuck into the workroom around noon to slide a plate of Ritz crackers and string cheese under my nose. She also stood behind me and delicately cleared her throat until I put aside my work. But she hadn't remembered to do that today, unfortunately, and my stomach complained with a loud gurgle.

I emerged from the workroom to find her standing by the cash register, counting sales receipts.

"Man, am I'm bushed." I rolled my shoulders as I walked over to her.

"Oh, hell's bells." She glanced up from the receipts. "I forgot to bring you lunch today, didn't I? You must be starving."

"Kinda. But maybe they'll have hors d'oeuvres at that auction preview."

She snapped her fingers. "That's right. My uncle always bragged about the food they served at those things. Said they also stocked an open bar to get people drunk and bidding like crazy."

"Good to know. Are you ready?"

"Almost done. We've had a big week and it's only Wednesday. You keep going like this and you can start taking Saturdays off."

Now that would be something. Everyone in the fashion industry looked forward to the day they could close up their studios on the weekends and enjoy a normal schedule like everyone else. But I needed a steady stream of referrals from wedding planners, dress designers, and personal shoppers to do that, which might take a while. In the meantime, I felt fortunate to get Sundays off, and sometimes even that didn't happen during wedding season.

"We'll see. I'm gonna freshen up a bit. Be right back."

I headed for the bathroom, where I found a tube of extra eyeliner, my favorite Chanel Rouge lipstick, and a plastic comb, which I used. Then I brought everything into the workroom and dropped them into a satin clutch I'd stashed in the bottom drawer of my desk. As an afterthought, I pulled the cell out of my pocket and slid it in there too. When I returned to the showroom, Beatrice was waiting for me by the front door.

"One more thing." I quickly scanned the studio before plucking up a cream picture hat with a demure pink hatband. "This one'll do." I would've preferred a zesty orange one to match my shift, but everything in my studio came in one of three colors: white, cream or whitish cream. Not one crazy color or loud pattern in the bunch. Although . . . I once had a biker bride who asked for a cherry-red bowler to go with a black ball gown, but that was a whole 'nother story.

Once finished, I flicked off the light and followed Beatrice through the doorway and into the parking lot. We walked by several studios—including Ambrose's, of course—until we reached the entrance to the atrium.

The glass pyramid was the crown jewel of our shopping center. Four sheer panes rose twenty feet in the air before meeting at the apex. Underneath the triangles of glass were white marble floors that held a Starbucks coffee bar, two public restrooms, and a sitting area with a Mies van der Rohe couch. A real one too; not a fake.

The rest of our building might have looked like a former spice factory, which it was, but the atrium reminded me of the pyramid at the Louvre. A security guard once told me the spice factory needed a tall center space for its bottling equipment and the architect simply substituted glass for brick during the building's remodeling.

It definitely looked like a museum tonight, with a dozen birchwood easels placed around the space as we walked in. A nearby table held bidding paddles and brochures, and directly across from it loomed the open bar Beatrice had warned me about.

Thankfully, tuxedoed servers moved through the small crowd with silver trays.

"Hallelujah," I said. "Time to eat."

"Think I'll mingle for a bit. I'm not really hungry and I want to see the auction stuff."

While Beatrice wandered away, I scanned the room. Several other tenants stood nearby, nibbling appetizers and gossiping. I noticed Bettina Leblanc right away, who owned Pink Cake Boxes. Bettina personally handed out samples every Tuesday and Friday afternoon . . . or so I'd been told.

Behind her sat a folding table loaded with DJ equipment and our very own DJ Freestylez. He'd forbidden us from using his real name, which was Francis, although sometimes we couldn't resist, since his face always pinked to high heaven whenever we did that. Tonight

Francis, aka DJ Freestylez, wore his headset half on and half off his head, which made him look like a mad scientist with a new experiment.

But enough with the people-watching . . . if I didn't eat something soon, DJ Freestylez would be playing a dirge at my funeral. I'd spied a particularly tempting appetizer tray ahead that held plain, instead of fried, spring rolls, so I followed the server until she came to a stop and then asked for one.

The minute I bit into the shrimp doused with lime juice and a touch of mint, I knew I'd made the right choice.

"Good, aren't they?"

I turned. Bettina smiled and lifted a half-eaten roll in greeting.

"Hm-mmm." I quickly swallowed.

"I love it when they leave the wrapper alone. I always say if God had wanted us to fry spring rolls, he wouldn't have made flour wrappers."

"You could be right. Course, I forgot to eat lunch again today. Almost anything would've tasted good at this point."

Bettina rolled her eyes. "You too? Can't believe how busy we've been this wedding season. I've baked over a hundred cakes since June. Not that I'm complaining, mind you, but I'd like to see my grandkids again."

It was easy to forget Bettina had grandchildren, since she looked so young. The first time I saw pictures of them in her bakery, I did a double take, mainly because she wore her shiny black hair in a ballerina bun and none of the strands were gray, as far as I could tell. She also scurried back and forth from the bakery to the parking lot like someone half her age. Many times she schlepped cake boxes out to a customer's car first thing in the morning and was still at it after nightfall.

"You should bring your grandkids around to the shop," I said. "I'm sure they'd love to help you out."

She chortled, which jiggled the appetizer in her hand. "They'd help me out, all right. They'd help me right out of my profits. Those rascals will lick a cupcake bald and slip it right back in the box." She leaned close. "They think I won't notice."

"I used to do that." For some reason, I'd lowered my voice too.

Thank goodness DJ Freestylez preferred soft Michael Bublé tunes over something louder.

"Or I took a bite out of every piece of chocolate until I found one with caramel."

"So you understand." She straightened. "Figure I can visit the kids in November, once wedding season is over."

When she popped the last of her appetizer into her mouth, I took a moment to scan the crowd. Groups of twos and threes milled around us with hors d'oeuvres and champagne glasses. Farther back stood the serious auction-goers, who hovered around the easels. Every once in a while, one waved over an attendant, who wore a navy blazer and linen gloves. Then the girl—or guy—stepped up like a tin soldier, clapped a thin piece of cardboard behind the item and another one in front, and then flipped the whole thing around like a pancake on a griddle. A girl did that twice before I noticed something else.

Bookending the line of easels were two cherrywood columns about five feet high, their shafts carved into perfect corkscrews. I knew enough about antiques to spot a curve made by a machine and not a wood-carver, but antique or not, they were still pretty. They'd look wonderful in Ambrose's studio, with its plaster-of-Paris cherubs, elegant dove-gray paint, and gilded mirror.

Speaking of which . . . where was he? Maybe I should've mentioned the preview to him over breakfast. Although, truth be told, Ambrose wasn't a huge fan of antiques, which surprised me to no end when I first met him. How could someone who designed a studio to look like a Parisian atelier *not* like antiques? It didn't make sense, but then again, not much about Ambrose did. Maybe that was why I liked him so much.

As soon as Bettina finished her spring roll, she wiped her lips with a cocktail napkin. "I need to use the ladies' room. See if you can try the crab puffs too. The server's over there by Francis. The cook went and fried 'em, but they're still tasty."

She scurried away, while I finished eating. Then I rubbed my oily fingers on a napkin and pondered my next move.

"Hello, there. Aren't you Beatrice's friend?"

I nearly dropped the napkin when a man spoke behind me. It sounded like Hank Dupre, Beatrice's uncle. So I turned and immediately blinked at the sight of so much purple and gold splayed across one shirt. The fleurs-de-lis collided with each other, all the way across his chest, shoulders, and arms. There were too many to count and too many for any one shirt.

"Um, hmmm." It was the most I could manage, given the circumstances. The last time I saw that pattern was at Miss Odilia's Southern Eatery, when he'd met with Ashley Cox for dinner. They'd been so chummy, they looked like old friends or, heaven forbid, new business partners.

Realization dawned on his face. "That's it. You're Bea's boss. You two borrowed my pirogue the other day. My niece sure has a strange sense of humor."

A thousand questions flittered through my mind, and none of them had anything to do with his boat. "You know, I think I saw you the other night." I did my best to sound casual. "You were at Miss Odilia's Southern Eatery. You and Ashley Cox, the guy who owns Sweetwater."

Was it my imagination, or did his jaw tense?

"Did you now? We had us a little business meeting. Nothing serious. I should probably stop taking people out to dinner there. Maybe then I'll lose this-here weight." He gave a forced chuckle.

"I had some questions for you, as a matter of fact." The most important one being whether Mr. Solomon really did own Sweetwater now. "I heard somebody up and bought the old Sweetwater mansion. But I couldn't imagine that was so, since the property doesn't have a real estate agent. Do you know anything about it?"

His jaw definitely clenched now.

If I hadn't spent time with him on our drive down to the river, I might've been a little frightened. "Mr. Dupre?"

"Just thinking, that's all. Look, I'd love to stay and chat with you, but I have to make a call. A . . . um . . . really important call."

He turned and dashed away. It was amazing how fast his mood had changed.

My stomach complained again with a loud rumble as he disappeared. *Lorda mercy.* One spring roll obviously wasn't going to cut it. I might as well get something else to eat, so I glanced around the room, seeking out the server from before, and found her by the row of easels.

When I reached her, her tray was half empty. While good manners dictated I should take a smaller one this time, it being my second helping and all, my stomach convinced me otherwise, and I scooped up the fattest one in the bunch. I backed away from the girl before starting in on it.

Cccrrraaassshhh! Something landed on the ground behind me with a sickening clatter.

Good Lord, what did I do?

I whirled around. An easel sprawled on the ground, next to something sheathed in layers of Mylar. At least half-a-dozen layers covered the document, no doubt to protect it from clumsy people like me.

Even with the wavering Mylar, I spotted an inked compass in the lower right-hand corner, which meant I'd apparently toppled over a map. And not just any map, either. The shimmering outline of Louisiana also appeared.

The document looked old and very valuable. No wonder I felt a hundred eyes on me as I dropped my appetizer and my purse to the ground and lurched forward.

But I was too late. An attendant in a navy blazer and thick glasses, who must've been waiting behind this particular easel, whooshed forward to sweep it off the ground. She was joined by a security guard, who moved almost as fast as she did.

Briskly, efficiently, the attendant ran a gloved finger along all four corners, while I held my breath.

After at least ten years, she smiled. It was a tight smile, but a smile nonetheless. "No harm done." She made the announcement to the crowd as if she'd been the one to topple the treasure and not me. Bless her heart.

"Thank goodness." I could've kissed her on the lips.

Now more attendants sprang into action. One stepped around the security guard to produce two boards, which he held open so the girl with the glasses could slip the map between them. Then she ferried the whole shebang to its original easel, which someone else had righted. Inch by inch, the attendant slid the map back into place, like a jeweler mounting a precious stone.

"I am *sooo* sorry," I said.

"Don't worry about it. It was an accident. These things happen."

Not knowing what else to do, I glanced down, where bits of lettuce and shrimp lay scattered around my purse. The spring roll must've burst open, so I bent and scooped the mess into my napkin, which I stashed in one of the clutch's pockets, before rising again. "Next time I'll pay more attention."

"Like I said, there was no harm done. Would you like to see the map?" Now the girl's smile looked genuine, which I appreciated even more.

"Yes, please."

She nodded to the security guard before starting in on the protective sleeves. She removed one sheath of Mylar after another, until all that remained was a map of the Great River Road. The delicate parchment rippled in spots, and time had faded the ink several shades lighter. The date scrolled across the top in sweeping, fanciful strokes was 1862.

"Wow. What a great piece. Made during the Civil War, right?"

The girl nodded briskly. "Yes, ma'am."

Since she'd just saved my backside, I tried not to notice she'd addressed me like a much older woman, even though we were both about the same age. "What are those marks along the river?"

She leaned in to get a better view. "The squares, ma'am? They show the location of the plantation homes around here."

"Really?" Now it was my turn to peer. About a dozen squares dotted the riverbanks of the Mississippi; some small, some large. I automatically sought out Bleu Bayou, which had four squares and a drawing of what looked like sugarcane. The largest square obviously stood for Morningside Plantation, since its fence line was enormous, compared to the others. A smaller square nestled near a curve could've been Sweetwater.

"Here. See this one?" My finger hovered over a spot under the wavering plastic, since I had no intention of ever touching the map again. "Does that look like an S next to it?"

She squinted. "It does. Let's check the legend."

We both stared at what could've passed for a legend, since it accompanied the compass, only the type was so fine and so small, it was impossible to read.

"Maybe the brochure will say." She pulled an auction catalog from the pocket of her blazer. "I'm not real good with these new glasses."

She held up the thin booklet, which had a picture of the map on its cover. Now I felt even worse, since she was going to so much trouble on my account.

"Sure enough." She looked at me. "The square is Sweetwater Plantation, and there's a star next to it. That meant a Confederate general had ordered his troops to hide ammunition there. The brochure says a plain square meant Confederates shouldn't stop, probably because the house belonged to a Union sympathizer or didn't have ammunition. But a star meant someone had stashed cannonballs, case shells, or grapeshot there. That's so cool! No wonder this thing costs so much."

The voices around me gradually softened. They were replaced by the memory of something hard and hollow—like a bowling ball, wasn't it?—that fell onto a floorboard at Sweetwater. It was a trapdoor, and Ambrose had leaned over it with a tailor's ruler in his hand, if I recalled correctly.

Ashley and I had come running from the kitchen to the foyer, only to find him there. While I'd been thrilled by the idea of a secret compartment, Ashley couldn't care less. Apparently his mother had installed the hiding place in the floor and then emptied it sometime before she died. That was what he'd said, anyway.

Only Ambrose didn't buy that story. Not when he found cast-iron hinges on the door instead of stainless-steel ones, which he seemed to think was a big deal.

"It's being offered by someone named H. Dupre," the attendant said. "And the bidding will start at one hundred and fifty thousand dollars." She softly whistled.

Shut my mouth and call me Shirley. Of course. Ambrose had known that hiding place was no accident. He could tell it'd been designed to hold something special; maybe even priceless. That was why Ashley's story didn't convince him.

For more than 150 years, people had tromped right over a Civil War treasure when they walked into Sweetwater. Maybe Ashley was going through his mother's things and found the map by accident. And maybe he'd heard that Hank Dupre knew all about the auctions around here. Was that how the two men got together?

And what about Mellette? Did she catch wind of their plan and threaten to expose them? What if she'd spied Ashley with the treasure, or had checked the hiding place one day and found it empty?

"Is something wrong, ma'am?" The attendant frowned at me.

"What? No, nothing. I was just remembering something."

I turned away from the gal. So many memories came flooding back. I'd walked across that very hall with Mellette, never once guessing what lay beneath our feet. Mellette had given me the grand tour and then paused by the dining room, where she motioned to a cottage on the other side of a large picture window. She'd called the cottage a "sweet hidey-hole." One of several hidden around the property, she'd said. It all made sense now.

I clumsily reached into my purse for my cell. I knew better than to approach Hank Dupre by myself, since I had no idea how he'd react. Better to call for reinforcements and get Lance out to the atrium.

I dialed his number and nervously tapped my foot until he answered.

"Hey, what's up? Better be important, 'cuz you're interrupting my dinnertime."

I lowered my voice, even though the attendant had disappeared. "You won't believe what's happened. I'm at the Factory, by my studio." Silence. "Lance?"

"I'm here. You're just freaking me out a little. What's wrong?"

I brought the cell even closer. "Remember what I said about Hank Dupre yesterday? He's a Realtor around here and my assistant's uncle. I saw him at your mom's restaurant the other night. With Ashley Cox, the guy who owns Sweetwater."

"Yeah, I remember. What does any of that have to do with you?"

"We're both at the same auction." I spoke quickly, willing him to understand. "An antique auction, and the big item for sale is a map from Sweetwater. I swear Hank Dupre and Ashley Cox took the map and now they're trying to sell it, only Mellette Babineaux found out about it. And, Lance?"

"Yeah, I'm still here."

"They want a hundred and fifty thousand dollars for the thing. That's just the opening bid. Don't you think it all makes sense?"

He exhaled loudly. "You're right. That's a lot of money. Okay, don't move. I'll come right over. Try to not go anywhere or say anything until I get there."

Relief washed over me. "We're all in the atrium. That's the big glass part in the middle of the Factory. You can't miss it. Hurry, okay?"

"You got it. Just hold on. And . . . Missy?"

"Yeah."

"I mean it. Don't do anything stupid."

"Roger that. I won't do anything until you get here. But you gotta hurry."

I hung up and returned the phone to my purse. Only a few minutes had passed since I'd spoken with Hank Dupre, so he couldn't have gone far. Although I'd promised Lance I wouldn't do anything stupid, that didn't mean I couldn't keep my eye on him.

Sure enough, he wasn't hard to spot in that ridiculous shirt. He'd moved to the table with the bidding paddles, beside the exit.

He leaned over the tabletop, as if looking for something. After a second he straightened and then spoke to a guy on his left. Not just any guy, either. This one had blond hair shaved at the sides and an enormous Rolex that glinted when he took a drink of champagne.

It was Ashley Cox. Waiting with Hank Dupre by the exit, only a few feet from the door.

Instinctively, I plunged my fist back into my purse and yanked out the cell. I began to punch in Lance's number, until doubt crept in. What good would it do to call him again? Nagging might only slow him down. So I let the phone slide back into place.

What I needed was a diversion. Something to keep the men away from that exit until Lance arrived. Even though their item hadn't come up for bid yet, one of them could decide to leave early.

Frantically, my eyes scanned the room, until I spied something tall and heavy and out of the way. It was one of the carved wood columns, placed at least three yards from the glass wall. I couldn't, could I?

I inched toward it, passing several easels on the way. The first one held an oil painting of a soldier wearing a tricorn hat. Next up was an antique bill of sale . . . for what, I couldn't say. I moved faster now, past four pen-and-ink drawings, until I finally reached the end of the line.

My eyes flew to the exit again. Sure enough, Hank and Ashley had moved even closer to the door. *It's now or never.* I pretended to yawn, and then I leaned heavily against the column, which swayed under my weight.

The pillar tottered back and forth, tantalizingly. Just when I thought it might actually topple over, it wobbled back into place.

So I tried again. This time I lifted my arms over my head as if to stretch, and then I threw my shoulder against the wood. Pain radiated down my arm, but the column gave way. All it took was one giant push for the momentum to send the pilaster falling to the ground.

Cccrrraaassshhh! Once again, the thunderous sound of something hard hitting marble rang out. Only this time, the entire room fell silent.

People stopped in the middle of their words to turn and stare. Especially since the column bounced against the marble once, twice, three times . . . before it finally began to settle on the ground.

Even the music stopped. I pretended to stagger backward and an attendant rushed forward to help me.

"Are you all right?" It was the same girl from before, who blinked behind heavy glasses when she realized it was me. "Oh my goodness. You could've been hurt this time."

I wobbled unsteadily as the column finally settled into place. Then I smacked my hand dramatically against my forehead. "Thash damn good champagne!"

The attendant was thunderstruck. She knew I wasn't drunk, since she'd spoken to me only a second before. But no one else knew that. Little by little, the sound of nervous laughter rippled through the crowd, especially when everyone realized I was unhurt.

"Get that girl some coffee!" a man yelled, as his buddies began to hoot and holler.

"Ish fine." I acted a bit more for the crowd, swaying this way and that. Luckily, several people moved forward to help me, which only made the scene look more real. Beatrice was first, who looked horrified, followed by Hank Dupre, who seemed more confused than anything else.

"Missy!" Beatrice glared at me. "What is wrong with you?"

Hank shushed her. "Don't yell at her, Bea. Not her fault they're pouring champagne like water." He draped his arm around my shoulders and led me over to the Mies van der Rohe couch, where I collapsed against the back cushion.

Hank jerked his head toward the Starbucks coffee bar. "Over there, Bea. See if they've got some coffee. Make it strong."

Beatrice parted the small crowd that'd gathered, and that was when I spied someone else. Ashley Cox stood on the periphery, his hands jammed into his pockets. He too looked more confused than alarmed.

"Youse got it all wrong." I pitched forward dramatically; so dramatically I almost fell headfirst off the couch. "I only had thish much." I pinched my thumb and finger together and then squinted through a sliver of space between them.

"Of course you did. Hold on a second, and we'll see what Bea gets you to drink."

"More champagne?"

He chuckled. "No, honey. No more champagne."

After a few more minutes of world-class acting, if I did say so myself, during which time I asked Hank to dance with me at least twice, I finally saw a blur of blue uniform rush into the atrium.

The minute Lance entered, the mood shifted. Gone were the cat-calls, snickers, and eye-rolls. Instead, the crowd took a giant step backward, as if everyone was making way for royalty.

To his everlasting credit, Lance didn't blink when he saw me pitching and swaying on the couch. My hair whipped around my face, since I'd lost my hat in the scuffle, not to mention my purse and even one of my shoes. But whether I was a hot mess or not, Lance didn't hesitate.

"Missy . . . Missy . . . Missy." He sauntered over, as if this wasn't the first time he'd found me drunk and it probably wouldn't be the last. "Looks like you've had a little too much fun."

"Now, don't you tell your mama 'bout dish." I brought my finger sloppily to my lips. "Dish is our li'l secret."

"All right, everyone." He spoke loudly to the crowd. "Looks like the show's over. You can all go back to your party."

When he moved to lift me from the couch, I jerked my head toward Hank.

Thankfully, Lance caught my drift. "Hey there, I could use some help. Let's get this girl away from all these people."

Hank moved forward to help, and this time he slipped his hand under my arm.

"I want him too." I jerked my chin at Ashley. "He ish so cute."

"We'll need you too," Lance said. "I can use all the help I can get."

Ashley grudgingly agreed, and together, the men hoisted me off the couch on the count of three. With Hank on one side and Ashley on the other, we tottered out of the atrium in an odd procession. Lance led the way like a drum major, while Hank and Ashley stiffly marched along beside me, trying to keep me upright. That was how we approached the door, when Beatrice suddenly ran up behind us, the missing hat and purse clutched in her hand.

"The coffee bar was closed," she said. "Sorry 'bout that, Uncle. But we have some coffee in our studio."

Bless her pea-pickin' heart. Little did Beatrice know how helpful she was being by suggesting that.

"Dash a great idea!" I swiveled my head from side to side. "Let's go to that schtudio-thingy."

Lance held open the front door and we all struggled through. Then he took the lead again, with the four of us on his heels. We lurched through the parking lot and past the studios that abutted the atrium. Soon we came to Ambrose's Allure Couture, but the light was off, hallelujah, and Ambrose was gone.

The minute we arrived at Crowning Glory and all tumbled inside, I dropped the act.

"Oh, thank God." I whirled on Ashley and Hank. "These are your guys, Lance."

No one spoke for a moment or two. Beatrice recovered enough to flick on the light, but that was about it.

Hank found his voice first. "What's going on? You're not drunk."

"Damn straight." I rose to my full height, which wasn't easy considering I only had one shoe. "I had to buy some time so you guys wouldn't leave. But I know what you did at Sweetwater."

"Huh?" Somehow Ashley had found his voice too, but it didn't seem to help. "I don't get it."

"Apparently there's a very special map on sale tonight," Lance said. "Does that ring a bell?"

"You're kidding, right?" Hank's eyes darted from me to Lance. "Of course it does. That's why we're here."

"So you admit you stole the map from Sweetwater?" I'd expected more of a fight, but they both looked incredibly calm.

"Look, I know where you're going with this," Hank said. "And it might take a while for me to explain everything."

Beatrice moved to the counter, where she placed my things and brought out two of our stools. She handed one to her uncle and the other to me. "I don't understand any of this. Are we talking about the map on the auction brochure?"

I nodded. "The very same. It's worth at least at least a hundred and fifty thousand dollars."

"You're kidding!"

"My guess is Mellette Babineaux knew about it." I sank onto the stool. "She probably would've turned these guys in."

"Of course she knew about it." Ashley had been so quiet, I'd almost forgotten he was there. "We talked about it, even."

"So you admit it?" I said. "You guys got rid of Mellette Babineaux so she wouldn't tell people about the map?"

"Whoa. Hold on." Hank slid onto the other stool. "That's not what he's saying. The map may be priceless, but it belonged to Ashley here. He and his brother are the rightful heirs."

"Ruby Oubre told me a museum wants to buy the house," I said. "Only because of the artifacts inside. Those things are priceless. You can't just up and sell 'em."

Hank somberly waved away my objection. "Unfortunately, he can. Here in Louisiana we have a little something called 'acquisitive prescription.' It means you get to keep anything you have in your possession for ten years or more. The exact words are *continuously* and *peaceably*."

"Acquisitive what?" Lance looked about as confused as I felt.

"Prescription," he said. "Other states have something similar called 'adverse possession.'" He turned to Lance now. "Basically, it's part of our civil code. The Cox family had that map for generations. Like it or not, the heirs can do anything they want with it."

"Heirs," I said. "Plural. What about the brother? Did he know what was going on?"

"Yes, he did." Hank nodded. "They asked me to sell it for them, but I couldn't go to the auction house without an affidavit. Both brothers had to sign it."

"You have the affidavit with you?" Lance asked.

"No, sir. It's back in my office." He slowly rose from the stool. "You two must've thought we snuck out to Sweetwater in the middle of the night to steal it."

"But what about the tapestry?" I asked. "There was a huge tapestry back at Sweetwater and it's missing too."

"The same thing," Hank said. "We put it up for auction to see what it'd bring."

Even though he'd explained everything so glibly, a few things still didn't add up. "But you brushed me off back there." I rose until we stood eye to eye. "You got all weird when I asked you whether Sweetwater had been sold. What was that about?"

"I'm supposed to be working for the brothers on the sly." He gave a resigned shrug. "Guess that didn't work out too well. A lot of people will be mad at us when they hear we're selling off the antiques. That's why Ashley and his brother hired me as a go-between. For both the house, now, and the treasures. The truth is that the boys need the money."

"Really?" That didn't make much sense. What about the Rolex and the sports car and a key ring from Yale?

"It's true." Ashley looked even younger now that he'd dropped the bravado. "There's nothing left. That's why we're selling the map . . . and the house."

"One last question." I glanced at Hank. "You're a Realtor, not an attorney. How'd you know about the civil code?"

"It comes up a lot around here. You'd be surprised." He gave a somber nod. "And I *do* have a law degree from LSU. Right now there's a big fight brewing over property rights on the Atchafalaya. People want to kick out the locals who claimed the land years ago. I'm trying to help them prove they've been on it for so long, it should belong to them. 'Course, none of the other real estate agents around here agree with me."

My gaze fell to the floor. "I guess I got you all wrong." While it pained me to admit it, I couldn't deny my horrible mistake. "I hope you can understand why I jumped to conclusions."

"I do. And I probably would've thought the same thing. It must have been a shock for you to see a map of Sweetwater going on sale tonight. Speaking of which . . . the auctioneer probably has it on the podium right about now."

I glanced up to see Ashley check the watch on his wrist, only this time he didn't make a big show out of it. "You're right. It's almost seven. Maybe we should go back and see what's happening."

"I'll go with you." Beatrice had moved away from the counter. Thankfully, she didn't sound upset, even though I'd blatantly accused her uncle of murder. "Are you coming, Missy?"

"No, I'm good. I think I'll stay here with my tail tucked between my legs for a bit."

She chuckled. "Whatever you want. Course, I can't believe you actually believed a Dupre would do something like that." She tsked her way to the front door. "Might have to teach you a thing or two about our family line."

"Sounds like it," I said. "And I'm *sooo* sorry for the confusion. I'll see you tomorrow, okay?"

"Of course." She moved to open the door, followed by Hank and Ashley.

The moment the three of them stepped through it, I turned to Lance. "All right. Let me have it."

"What? You were only following your gut. I can see why you'd get upset about the map. Especially when you're talking about that kind of money."

"But my gut instinct was wrong, if you haven't noticed."

"It only means you'll have a better shot at being right the next time."

"Next time?"

"Sure. I still want you to help me. You've been in on this from the beginning. And don't forget you were right about the murder at Morningside. You're due for another win."

"Lord, I hope so." Come to think of it, maybe I should've gotten drunk on champagne at the antique auction, after all. Then I would've had a good excuse for my behavior.

"You can't beat yourself up." Lance kept up the chatter, no doubt hoping to cheer me up. "As a matter of fact . . . why don't we go get us something to eat? My treat. And if we visit my mom's place, it'll be on the house."

"You're kidding, right?" I sagged against the counter, suddenly exhausted by the weight of the day. "That sounds wonderful. And maybe I can blame my craziness on my empty stomach."

Chapter 17

I didn't say much on our drive over to Odilia's restaurant. Instead, I hunkered down in the passenger seat of Lance's Olds and thought about all of the people I'd talked to over the past few days. People like Hank, Ashley, Ruby, and Hollis. Somewhere along the line I'd taken a wrong turn, but where?

Hallelujah, Lance didn't feel the need to keep up the chatter now, although, every once in a while, I caught him sneaking a sideways glance at me.

"Do you want to talk about it?" he finally asked.

We'd arrived at the restaurant, where a steady stream of cars cruised in and out of the parking lot.

"There's not a whole lot to say. I feel like I've missed something. The right clue is out there. I just can't put my finger on it."

Lance made a hard left and pulled up behind an SUV waiting to enter the lot. "At least we can eliminate two suspects. That's something."

"I suppose." I'd waited for him to rib me about my mistake sometime during the drive. But he'd said nothing. Zip. "What's with the silence? I thought you'd give me a hard time."

He shrugged. "Can't say, really. But you seem to be beating yourself up pretty good all on your own. No need for me to do it too."

"Here's the thing: I'm worried I disappointed you."

"Disappointed?" Lance maneuvered the car into a parking space in the last row. "No, of course not. I'm not disappointed. Why would I be disappointed in you?"

"Because I've totally botched it. Here I thought I'd give you the answer about Mellette's murder all wrapped up, like a shiny present, for goodness sakes. Ta-da! Only it didn't turn out like that."

He set the car in *park* and slowly withdrew the keys. "There's your problem. Working an investigation isn't about making the clues fit what you think happened. It's the other way around. And sometimes even the clues can be wrong. Wasn't it Maya Angelou who said sometimes the facts obscure the truth?"

I arched an eyebrow. "You're quoting poets now? When did that happen?"

"Hey, I read." He unbuckled his seat belt. "Maybe it's time for a fresh perspective."

"But it's been three whole days." I reluctantly unbuckled my seat belt too. "Don't you think that's a long time for her family and friends to wait?"

"Not really. People have waited a whole lot longer than that." He swung open his car door and then stepped onto the pavement.

I did the same, lifting my feet over my purse and smashed hat that lay on the floorboard. Thankfully, the air outside had cooled, and a light breeze wafted around me as I slammed the car door shut. "So where do we go from here?"

"I don't know about you, but I'm getting something to eat. I've got a feeling it's going to be a long night."

Lance met me at the back of the Olds and took my arm. "Plus, you already said you get a little crazy on an empty stomach."

I couldn't fault his logic, so I walked with him through the parking lot and into the restaurant. Once again, a line of people snaked up to the hostess stand. Two teenaged girls stood there tonight, both dressed in black.

"You know," Lance said. "I could pull rank and get us a table right away."

"No thanks. I've been there and done that. I don't mind waiting."

"At least let me grab you a menu. My mom adds new things all the time. She's been going on and on about something called hummingbird cake."

He left to find a menu, and my eyes swept over the people ahead of me. Most of them were young couples, with not a baby, toddler or even a preteenager in sight. Which wasn't surprising, given that it was already past seven.

Lance returned a moment later, his hands empty. "Sorry, but she's not giving me a choice. The hostess up there knows me, and she wants to seat us right away."

Not again. "Seriously? Aren't you gonna be embarrassed to walk past all these people?"

"She said she'll take us the back way." He shot me a funny look. "Said you already know how to get there. What's that about?"

"She's right." The girl must've been working on Tuesday night, when I trailed behind Charles as he led Ambrose and me through the kitchen. "Okay. Sounds like I don't have any choice."

We waited for the hostess to find us, and then we followed her out of the restaurant. Thankfully, only a few people noticed us leave.

Once we navigated the stoop, we passed the pretty flower boxes on the wall, and then we turned the corner. A fan of light spread evenly over the grass by the employees' entrance, thrown there by a motion detector.

"Hey, that's new." I pointed at it.

"Sure is. I told you, she adds new things all the time."

Also new was the back door to the restaurant, which stood half open tonight. At least that meant the hostess wouldn't have to fight with it, like Charles had done. He'd been so hard-pressed to wrangle it open, I'd wondered if maybe he would give up.

A lone figure loitered by the new door. Caught between light and shadows like that, though, I couldn't quite see who it was.

A few more steps and I had my answer. Especially since the woman wore her gray hair in a messy ponytail, which she'd feathered over one shoulder.

"Hey, it's Ruby Oubre," I whispered loudly.

"So it is."

She looked disheveled tonight, her apron rumpled and stained.

"Hello there, Miss Ruby," I said.

She glanced up. "Evenin'." She sounded unsure, but her eyes widened when she saw Lance. "That you, Lieutenant?"

"Sure is, Miss Ruby."

"Whatcha doin' here?"

"We're trying to get inside. It's my mom's restaurant."

She suddenly pulled away from the wall. "Hey, I know ya two." She held a lit cigarette between her fingers, which she pointed at me. "You da one done tole me not ta worry 'bout ma dog. Gah-lee . . . ya was right. He came back!"

"That's great!" The last time we met, both Ruby's dog and her grandson had gone missing. "Did Hollis come back too?"

She nodded eagerly. "Shore 'nuff. Dat boy gonna be da death of me yet. 'Less I kill him first." Her chuckle was raspy and dry.

"So glad to hear they're both back."

The hostess waited for me to finish, no doubt eager to seat us and get back to work.

"Here, I'll take the menus," I told the girl. "I know how to get to the dining room from here."

"Cool." She gratefully passed them to me. "I've gotta get back up front or the manager will think I'm goofing off."

"Where do you want us to sit?"

"Table twelve. It's on the wall, about halfway back." She turned and began to hurry away, speaking over her shoulder. "Should be the only one open."

"Thanks." I tucked the menus under my arm and eyed Ruby again. "I didn't expect to see you here. Are you working at Odilia's now?"

"Yep." She took a long, slow drag from the cigarette. When she exhaled, a wisp of smoke curled away. "Deys need help wit da dishes. Ain't ma cuppa tea, but whatcha gonna do?"

"Good for you," Lance said. "I wondered what would happen to you when we closed off Sweetwater. I'd hoped you'd find another job."

"I'm jus' here for a li'l bit. Ma neighbors done take up a collection for some fancy lawyer outta Baton Rouge. He's gonna help us wit' da land. Gotta pay ma fair share."

She must've been talking about that "acquisitive prescription" thing Hank Dupre had explained as he sat on a stool in my studio. The way he told it, a group of locals had banded together to convince the government to give them some land. And not just any land: the land along the Atchafalaya. "I heard all about that. Hank Dupre said you guys are staking a claim to the riverbank."

She nodded at the name. "Dat's da fella goin' ta help us. Lotsa other folks wouldn't. Deys tole us we outta back off."

"How do you think it'll end up?"

The longer I talked, the more Lance drummed his fingers against the leg of his trousers, no doubt impatient for me to wind things up. But table twelve could wait, the way I figured it.

"Hard ta say. We gonna fight, though."

Finally Lance gave up and moved to the kitchen door, which he opened all the way. A wash of bright light overwhelmed the slimmer glare cast by the security device. "You do that, Miss Ruby," he said.

"I'm afraid we need to get inside now, or they're gonna give away our table."

"Let me know how it turns out, though," I said. "And I'm so glad your grandson—and your dog—came home."

She nodded her thanks. "Shore 'nuff. An' I made a gris-gris for dat lawyer up in Baton Rouge. Jus' in case."

No doubt. I patted her elbow as I walked past her and into the kitchen. Like before, I heard the sounds of people working long before I actually spotted them. Plates clattered, serving spoons thunked against metal, and voices barked out orders. A server in a crisp white dress shirt finally rushed past me, lightly grazing my elbow with a steaming plate of grits.

Lance was already in the thick of things, working his way past the prep area, toward the swinging door. I started to follow him, when I noticed a familiar face.

There, at the edge of the hubbub, stood Charles, wearing faded jeans, an LSU T-shirt, and running shoes. Whatever was Charles doing at the restaurant without his apron, not to mention the dish towel he always wore over his shoulder?

"Charles?" I practically yelled, but he didn't hear me. He looked confused as he vaguely studied the room. "Charles?" I repeated.

That did the trick. His gaze locked on mine as he stepped away from the wall. "What are you doing here?" he asked.

He looked haggard again. Blue-black shadows ringed both eyes and his hair fell greasy and lank.

"I'm having dinner here. The hostess insisted we take a table right away."

"Well, I don't have time to talk." His eyes dully roamed the kitchen. "I just came to pick up my last paycheck."

"Don't tell me you're leaving the restaurant?"

He nodded vaguely. "Yeah. It's not really my thing. Too many hours. You know how it goes."

"Sure," I said, although something about Charles seemed off tonight. He looked distracted, confused. "Are you okay?"

"Fine." His gaze returned to me. "Though I could use your help with something." He tentatively reached for my elbow, before easing me to the back of the kitchen, where another door stood. He stopped there. "I need you to give someone a message."

He motioned to the door and I followed him into a short hall, which was obviously part of the original house. Unlike the kitchen, which was hot and bright and raucous, the hall was cool and dim.

When first built, the hall led to three different rooms. Two of the doorways had been plastered over, although faint ridges remained under the drywall, while a third door was still in use.

Charles dropped my elbow and made his way to the closed door. After flinging it open, he reached for a ball chain that dangled from a bare bulb, which he pulled. I peeked into the space to see wire racks filled with cleaning supplies.

I remained in the hall, though. He seemed confused tonight and I couldn't imagine what Charles would want to ask me.

His hand waved around listlessly. Everything from gallon jugs of Dawn dish soap to packs of snowy water-softener pellets and paper-towel rolls packed the shelves. The top one even held a neon bucket with pink gloves draped around its lip like flower petals.

"This is where Ruby has to get her stuff. Not much to look at."

"Did you say something about a message?"

His hand fell to his side. "Look, a lot of people don't know this . . . but I'm going away. I need you to tell Beatrice something. She was supposed to meet me here tonight. Guess she never checked her phone."

Beatrice? True, the two of them had worked together at Morning-side and they'd dated off and on for a few months, but Beatrice had insisted she never wanted to see him again. Something about him being too moody. I didn't push her for an explanation and she never did offer one.

But first things first. "I'm sorry it didn't work out here. How did Odilia take the news?"

He shifted his weight impatiently. "Fine, I guess. Anyway . . . tell Beatrice I had to go, but I'll call her soon."

"I thought you two weren't dating anymore." As a matter of fact, Beatrice went so far as to make up a plan in case Charles ever showed up at our studio unannounced. She was going to hide in the workroom and wait for me to stomp my foot three times to signal the all-clear. I thought she was being silly at the time.

"She'll come around. She doesn't know what she wants right now." Charles's eyes narrowed and I could see why Beatrice might need that plan, after all.

Before he could say more, a noise sounded at the end of the hall.

Someone had banged open the door to the kitchen, and their shadow fell across the floor as they entered the hall. A whiff of cigarette smoke preceded Ruby, who paused and clasped her hand against her heart.

"*Zut alors!* Ya done scare me ta death. Didn't expect nobody ta be back here."

"Hello, again," I said. "Charles and I were just having a little chat."

"Are ya now?" Ruby exhaled loudly. "Shame on ya for scarin' an ol' lady like dat."

"I'm sorry. We didn't mean to frighten you. But Charles had something to ask me, and you know how loud that kitchen is."

She eyed me suspiciously. "I didn' even know ya two was friends."

"We met back at Morningside Plantation," I said. "Charles was my waiter. Probably the best one I've ever had."

"Look, I gotta go." Charles spoke quickly now. "My plane—"

"Dat's right." Recognition sparked behind Ruby's watery eyes. "You two was together at Sweetwater da other mornin'."

"Other morning?"

"Monday," she said. "Member dat? I saw ya and thought ya was bad news 'cuz ya come callin' on da first a da week and women bring da bad luck den. Da look on your face." She gave another raspy chuckle. "Gah-lee."

"How could I forget that?" I echoed her laughter. "You wouldn't even let me in the front door. Thank goodness Mellette was there to open it for me."

"I never tol' Charles here." She cut her eyes at him. "But dat's when I saw ya both. Ya was lookin' around on yer own, but I done figure ya come together. So I knew ya was friends."

Come to think of it, I remembered standing in Ruby's dusty living room, back at her mobile home, after Ambrose and I had stumbled upon Mellette's body in the garden shed. Ruby told me she'd seen me with a man at Sweetwater that morning, but I'd always assumed she meant Ambrose.

"I brought my friend to Sweetwater for a tour," I explained. Poor Ruby must have been so confused by the murder she mistook Ambrose for Charles. "That's probably who you saw me with that day."

She shook head adamantly. "I know what I'm talkin' bout. No way ta miss dat head of hair." She jerked a thumb at Charles.

The longer we talked, the closer to us Charles had edged, until now he stood in the hall with us. Ruby was right: that salt-and-pepper hair was gray enough for a man twice his age. "Charles?"

He lunged forward. Before I could move, he shoved his palms against Ruby's back and sent her sailing toward me. Together we toppled into the closet, and a wire shelf bit painfully into my shoulder. Buckets, gloves, and bottles rained down as the shelf banged against the wall.

I barely had time to raise my arms over my head before an enormous bottle of Dawn came crashing down. The hailstorm continued for a few seconds, while Ruby shivered against me.

Everything seemed darker by the time it ended and then I realized why: Charles had slammed the closet door shut. The falling debris must have muffled the sound. We were trapped inside the jumble of overturned buckets, sprays of dishwashing soap, and scattered paper-towel rolls.

I gently pushed Ruby aside and reached for the doorknob ... which was locked.

What was worse: Feeling Ruby cower next to me in fear, or the shock of realizing I'd forgotten my cell phone in Lance's car?

"Oh, sweet Jesus," I said. "You know what this means, right?"

Ruby whimpered instead of answering me.

"It means Charles is the one who killed Mellette Babineaux." I steadied my voice for her sake, but my heart beat faster now. "He knew I figured it out and he panicked. Think about it—he was there that morning. He told me he hated some of the Realtors around here. The ones who wouldn't help the locals. I should have known. I should've . . ."

Beating myself up wasn't going to do anyone a lick of good. What we needed was a plan; a way to get out of the closet and find Lance before it was too late.

I grasped Ruby's shoulder. "Okay, we need to think. There must be a way out of here."

She flinched when I touched her. "But dere ain't no other way."

"What about a vent? Maybe an air-conditioning vent that leads outside?"

"Dis room be hotter den a stove. Dere's no vent."

Quickly I scanned the room. Heaven only knew how far Charles had traveled by now. He could be halfway across town while we cooled our heels in a ransacked storage closet.

After a moment, Ruby straightened. "But dere's sumptin' else."

"What? What did you say?"

"Dere's another way." She stepped out from under my grasp and peered at the shelf, now leaning all catawampus behind us.

"What way?" I knew better than to yell, but we were running out of time. "Tell me what way!"

She pointed at it. "Behind dere. 'Bout as high as yer head."

I followed her eyes. Most of the shelf lay bare, since everything had tumbled to the ground, but a box of rubber gloves, some Clorox bleach, and a toilet plunger with a wooden handle, all of which I pushed aside to clear a path to the wall.

Like the two doors in the hall, someone had drywalled over an opening here. Only this opening was much smaller: maybe two feet wide by two feet high, at the most. Which would give me just enough room to wiggle through it, if I could only knock out the drywall.

"I found it!" I turned around again. "What was it?"

"Dis used to be da kitchen. Dat's where da man unloaded da ice blocks."

Praise the Lord we live in the hot South! I'd heard stories about old kitchens and how a cook ordered a block of ice from a delivery-man. The iceman scooted the block through a special hole that led straight to a wood box. Packed with ice on the top shelf, the food below it cooled, which was no easy feat during the hot summer months.

"You're brilliant!' I reached over to hug her, and this time she didn't flinch. "Here, help me move the shelf away."

With Ruby at one end and me at the other, we tugged the shelf away from the wall. Since almost everything on it was gone now, it easily slid aside.

I scooped up the plunger from the floor and grasped the wood handle. Using it as a battering ram, I struck it against the drywall over and over again, until bits and pieces of paper and plaster began to fall out. When the progress slowed, I clawed at the opening with my bare hands, pulling out chunks of gypsum board until bright light eked through a pinhole opening.

I glimpsed some tables at the other end of the pinhole. Come to think of it, there was no need for me to make the opening larger. Not when I had a perfectly good set of lungs on me.

"Help!" I yelled through the hole. "We're locked in here."

Ruby joined me and together we created quite a chorus. A few seconds later, something scuffled on the other side of the closet door.

"Missy!" It was Lance. "I'm here."

I ran over to the door. "Thank God! We can't get out."

"Who did this to you?" Even muffled by an inch of wood, his voice shook with anger.

"It was Charles. He's the one who killed Mellette Babineaux. He panicked when I figured it out."

"Charles?" Lance fell silent as he pondered my response. "You're sure?"

"Positive. And he's getting away."

"Okay. Stay calm. And move away from the door." Lance had switched to his official-sounding police voice, which I used to find irritating but now found heavenly.

Ruby and I both hugged the back wall as Lance began to strike the doorknob. He must have pulled his sidearm out of its holster and used the butt of it. Like a hammer hitting a nail head, the noise boomed in the quiet. After two tries, the brass knob clunked to the ground and the door swung open.

Lance quickly holstered his gun and rushed to us, arms extended, as if we'd been locked in the closet for days.

"We're okay." I tried to reassure him, but he continued to fuss. "Charles didn't hurt us. He just trapped us in here so he could get away."

Finally, Lance must have believed me and took a step back. "Don't worry, he can't get far. I'm just glad nothing happened to you."

"You and me both."

"I'm gonna call the station. What kind of car does Charles drive?"

"I'm not sure," I said. "My assistant will know, though."

"Okay. Get in touch with her while I call my sergeant." He paused, his voice softening ever so slightly. "And I'm really glad nothing happened to you."

I arched an eyebrow. "Now don't get all soft on me, Lance. Ruby and I are fine. And we've got to find Charles before it's too late."

Ruby softly tsked as she hobbled out of the closet first. "None a dis had ta happen, ya know."

"What?" I touched her shoulder to stop her. "What do you mean?"

She half-turned and cocked her head. "If'n ya had yer gris-gris wit you, dis mighta not happened."

"Oh, Miss Ruby." I grinned, so relived to be following her into the hall. "You don't really believe that, do you?"

"Maybe I do an' maybe I don'. But ya ain't gonna know 'til ya try it."

She had a point. I followed her as she turned and made her way down the hall, inhaling deeply with each step. Amazing how thin the air had become once the door was slammed shut. Even the walls had closed in on me, squeezing oxygen out of the space. Now I could finally breathe again, and I flung my arms wide open as I walked behind Ruby.

But my joy was short-lived. I still needed to phone Beatrice, after all, who had hopefully remained at the studio. She could give me the make of Charles's car. I picked up the pace as I strode through the kitchen and then made my way to the employee entrance. No one seemed to notice me, or, if they did, no one tried to stop me.

I reached Lance's car within a few seconds. There, lying on the floorboard of the front seat, was my cell phone. Thank goodness Lance hadn't bothered to lock his doors, which I would tease him about later, and Beatrice soon came on the other end of the line when I dialed her number.

I told her my story in a rush of words, since we had so much to do. And this time none of the facts obscured the truth, no matter what Maya Angelou might have said.

Chapter 18

The moment Ambrose pulled up to Commander's Palace in New Orleans, my breath stalled. How in the world did a Gulf wave manage to breach the levee and stop at the corner of Washington and Coliseum streets in the Garden District?

That was exactly what the Victorian mansion in front of us looked like: a blue wave frozen on a corner, surrounded by live oaks, crisscrossed telephone wires, and waxy magnolia bushes.

"It's so beautiful," I murmured.

Ambrose smiled as we drove up to the valet stand. Even with all the hullabaloo surrounding Mellette's death and Charles's arrest, he'd insisted on keeping our date. "I knew you'd like it. A lot of people can't get past the blue paint."

True, every shingle, plank, and doodad on the second floor of the restaurant wore the same shade of French blue. But the never-ending color dribbled away into just one half of a blue-and-white stripe by the time it reached the ground. The striped awning ran around the entire bottom floor, from front to back.

"I think it's quirky," I said. "And that's not a bad thing."

"You've got your pick of stories about the place." Ambrose slid the Audi into *park* and waited for the valet to open my door. "It was either a wedding gift for the builder's daughter, or it used to be a bar."

I mulled the two options. "Tell me the story about the wedding gift first. That's much more romantic."

Ambrose leaned away from the steering wheel. "Supposedly Emile Commander was only twenty-two when he built his restaurant, right across from a cemetery. People talk about seeing his ghost sometimes, always standing by the bar, since he was a big drinker. There's another ghost, a girl, who may or may not be his daughter.

She never married, apparently, and she haunts the staircase looking for her lost love."

"Ooohhh, that's creepy. I like it. What about the saloon story?"

"That one's not as fun. Other people think the guy built a saloon across the way, and since the Civil War was over, immigrants started flooding the city. The French Creoles in town didn't want 'em, so they kinda adopted the bar as their meeting place."

"You're right. That's not as fun. Let's go with the ghosts instead."

By now the valet had arrived at Ambrose's window, so he hopped out and joined me by the front door. We walked into a lobby that was every bit as eclectic as the outside of the building.

A cut-out panel of iron scrolls allowed me to peek into the dining room. The walls were papered in violet and gold, and above them hung wood chandeliers laced with strings of crystals that dipped and swirled through unshaded bulbs. Even higher flowed a white ceiling—as pristine as the linen-clad tables—edged with thick crown molding that circled the room like a crisp hatband.

I immediately sighed. "It's perfect."

"Good evening." A maître d' greeted us with a stiff bow, which he relaxed when he saw Ambrose. "Why, hello Mr. Jackson. I didn't realize it was you. So nice to see you again."

"Likewise," Ambrose said. "Table for two, please. It's under my name."

I threw up my hands as we followed our host into the dining room. "I should've known you'd be on a first-name basis with the staff," I said in a stage whisper. "Let me guess . . . you're best friends with the sommelier too?"

"Maybe. Depends on who's working tonight." Ambrose took over hosting duties when we reached the table and gallantly pulled my chair away. "I promised you a special night. Trust me. The food here won't disappoint."

I stifled a grin. Little did Ambrose know I would've been happy with a Whopper from Burger King. For after a year and a half of platonic friendship, during which time I'd spun too many daydreams about him to count, he'd finally asked me out on a real, honest-to-goodness date.

Of course, other men had come around during that time, but they never seemed to measure up. To hear Beatrice tell it, it was because I never gave them a chance. But I knew all along I'd be wasting my time, so why bother?

Especially after seeing Ambrose tonight, which made my heart flip-flop. Tonight he'd paired his gray Armani suit with an aqua tie that made his blue eyes pop. He'd also slicked his hair back, my favorite style for him.

For my part, I'd put aside the Lilly Pulitzer shifts for once and picked up an "lbd" by Chanel. This "little black dress" originally cost more than a thousand dollars, but I'd paid only a hundred for it at a place called the Recycled Rag in town.

The sleeveless dress featured a sheer bodice that ended with a high-necked lace collar. Black teardrop earrings and Chanel Rouge lipstick completed the ensemble. My goal was to channel Audrey Hepburn, which must've worked, since Ambrose kept staring at me.

"What's wrong?" I finally asked him. "Do I have something on my face?"

He leaned across the table. "Nothing I haven't seen a million times before. You look wonderful tonight."

Instead of responding like a grown-up should, a giggle formed at the back of my throat, which I desperately tried to stifle.

He shot me a funny look when it came out anyway. "Maybe we should start with a drink."

"Definitely." I gulped. "That sounds good."

"I'll choose for us, if you don't mind."

Hallelujah, a sommelier arrived at our table with a wine menu, which she offered to Ambrose. After reading it, he passed it back to her and murmured something or other. Say what you will about feminism, but I was more than happy to have Ambrose select the bottle, since he actually cared about things like vintages and provenances and winemakers. The last time he ordered for us, he'd selected a crisp Chardonnay, which I'd thoroughly enjoyed, although he'd mentioned it wasn't his favorite type of wine.

"Like I was saying . . . you seem to know the staff here," I said. "Take many girls along?"

"Only one." When I didn't respond, he added, "I meant you, of course. Usually I come here for business meetings. My clients and I like to meet over lunch."

"You're lucky." Maybe now would be a good time to steer the

conversation onto neutral ground, since it'd finally give me a chance to get past his beautiful blue eyes. "By the way—did you hear what happened yesterday at the police station?"

"No, I didn't. I just hope they threw the book at Charles. He could've hurt you, you know."

"But he didn't." I took a sip of water, relieved to put the awkwardness behind us. "No one ever suspected he was the one who killed Mellette Babineaux."

"Did something new happen, then?"

"It did." He waited while I took another sip of water. "They got a preliminary toxicology report back."

"But I thought that usually takes weeks."

"Normally it does." Even Lance was surprised by the quick turnaround on this one. "They gave Lance a preliminary because of a tip. Ruby Oubre noticed something strange yesterday. Something she found in her garden."

"And she only noticed it now?" He looked confused, which was understandable. Since most plants took weeks to grow, Ruby must have lived right next to this one for quite some time.

I nodded. "It's not the best-kept plot of land. Anyway, Charles had snuck something in there called 'jack-in-the-pulpit.' Hid it between the other plants. It just takes a little bit mixed in with food to poison someone."

"I get it . . . so the medical examiner knew what to test for."

"Bingo. And jack-in-the-pulpit affects the kidneys and lungs. Mellette basically suffocated in the garden shed."

Ambrose winced. "What a horrible way to go. But how'd he get her to eat it?"

"That's the thing." I leaned forward. Even though no one else was nearby, it didn't feel right to broadcast the details of a police investigation to a roomful of strangers. "He must have told her he'd brought her something to eat from the restaurant. Probably something for breakfast, since it was so early. The medical examiner found the poison in the fluid of her lungs."

"You're right—she probably never suspected a thing."

"He knew exactly what he was doing. He picked something that grows well in these parts, and there's no odor to it, so Mellette wouldn't have known. He'd planned everything out to a T."

Ambrose frowned. "And he did all that because she was trying to get the locals to give up their land? Sounds kind of extreme."

"That's what I thought. But he has a history with the people who live along the bayou. Apparently they took care of him when his family went broke. But it's still no excuse for what he did."

Thankfully, the sommelier appeared at our table just then with two wineglasses and a bottle full of something claret-colored. She poured a sample for Ambrose, who tried it before nodding his approval, and then she filled my glass.

Ambrose raised his drink by the stem. *"Salud y amor y tiempo para disfrutarlo."*

I furrowed my brow. "Translation, please?"

"Here's to health and love and the time to enjoy it. In Spanish."

"That's perfect."" I took a long sip and tasted cherries and licorice. "Ummm. This is good."

"It's a cab from the Bordeaux region. I don't suppose you remember what I told you the other night?" Ambrose carefully set his glass down again.

"The other night?"

"Never mind. It'll sink in." His smile dimmed a bit. "There's one last thing I don't understand."

"What's that?" I took another sip and held the wine on my tongue a second longer.

"Why did Charles put a cross, of all things, near Mellette Babineaux's body?"

"Ah, the cross." I ran my finger around the lip of my glass while my thoughts receded to Monday. I'd never seen Ambrose so shaken before, which had made me weak-kneed. Especially when he told me about the cross and how the killer had smeared fresh blood on it. "That's another smart thing Charles did. He used chicken blood. He knew we'd waste time focusing on the bloody cross, instead of him. He thought he'd be long gone by the time we figured out the killing had nothing to do with voodoo. I guess we all underestimated him."

"Then I'm glad he's in prison." Ambrose lifted his wineglass again. "But enough about him. I think you deserve a vacation after all of this. I was thinking—"

Just then someone appeared at our table. She wore a black military-style jacket and huge hoop earrings, so I knew she wasn't part of the waitstaff. The twentysomething also held an iPad in her hand instead of a regular notepad.

"Aren't you Ambrose Jackson?" Her pixie face was hopeful.

"I'm sorry—do I know you?"

I shrugged when Ambrose glanced my way. I'd never seen the girl before, but she seemed anxious to speak with him.

"I knew it was you. I write a fashion blog. It's called *Southern Comforts*. Maybe you've heard of it?" She reached into her jacket and produced an orange business card. "Anyway, I've been to all of your shows. All of them. They're brilliant."

Ambrose gallantly accepted the card. "Thank you very much." He motioned to me. "But I'm on a very special date tonight. Maybe you could call next week, when I'm back in the studio."

The girl's face fell. "But I only wanted to ask you a few questions. Two, maybe three. A quick picture, and then I'll be gone. Poof! You won't even know I was here."

"That may be . . . uh—"

"Antonella," she said.

"That may be, Antonella, but I'm here for a special occasion. I'll tell you what . . ."

My eyes widened as he leaned back. Was Ambrose really going to interrupt our dinner to do an interview for a fashion blog? And not just any blog, but one written by a stranger who'd hijacked our date without any warning?

". . . I've got an idea," he said.

The girl stepped closer, obviously thrilled to have run into someone like Ambrose Jackson by accident.

"You can't be serious, Bo." The room around me began to warm, or was it the wine?

He shot me a look I couldn't quite read. "This is Missy DuBois. She's the story you want, not me."

"Excuse me?" The girl swiveled her pretty head, her brows furrowing. "You're a fashion designer too?"

"She's a milliner." Ambrose sounded pleased. "One of the best. She's been in all the top magazines." He winked at me slyly.

Bless his little heart. We both knew the only magazine I'd ever graced was stuck between pages of the *Bleu Bayou Impartial Reporter* on Sundays. But it didn't seem to matter, because the girl's eyes widened at the mention of another magazine.

"Cool. Let me log on real quick."

The girl—Antonella—flipped open the cover of her iPad, no doubt ready to start taking notes, when I held up my hand.

"That won't be necessary." Much as I appreciated Ambrose's sweet gesture, this wasn't the time or the place for it.

She glanced away from her device. "But it'll only take a second. Promise. The site's got thousands of readers. Some ads, even. Wanna see it?" She thrust the iPad toward me.

"I'm sure it's a wonderful site." I didn't take the bait. "And I'd love to do an interview with you. Just not now. Why don't you call me on Monday?" I reached into my clutch and withdrew an embossed business card for Crowning Glory, which I gave her.

Ambrose's wineglass hovered in midair, as if he didn't quite believe what he was hearing. But as much as I needed the publicity, I wanted to know where the two of us stood even more. And that couldn't happen with a stranger standing by our table.

"Are you sure?" he asked.

"Positive."

The girl reluctantly snapped her iPad's cover closed. "Okay. I'll call you then."

"And I just finished a project for one of the Prudhommes out of New Orleans," I said. "They're a big deal around here. I can send you pics from the fitting."

She looked uncertain as she began to back away. "Sure . . . um . . . whatever."

She slunk away, her shoulders slumped and her footsteps much slower now.

"Uh-oh," I said as soon as she was gone. "I think I burst her bubble."

"She'll get over it. But I've gotta warn you . . . sometimes these people don't give you a second chance. She might not call you Monday."

I leaned back. "That's okay. But thank you for giving me the chance."

"Look, there's something else I've been wanting to talk to you about." He rested his hands on the table, his face suddenly serious. "How about—"

At that moment, someone else approached us, only this stranger wore a black vest and matching wraparound apron.

Dagnabbit!

"Good evening." The waiter presented me a menu with a flourish, which I grudgingly accepted, and then I waited for him to give one to Ambrose, as well.

I gave a cursory glance to the dinner offerings. "Since you're the regular around here, I'll need some advice. You must have a favorite . . . even if you're usually here for lunch."

"I do." His eyes flittered over the menu. "You should try the turtle soup. And we'll definitely have bananas Foster for dessert."

Once the waiter took our order, I moved closer to the table. "Anyway, you were saying . . . ?" I tried my best to sound nonchalant.

"Was I? Let's enjoy dinner first."

Everything moved along in a blur after that: a wash of soft music, shared dinner plates, and lighthearted conversation. Since the person responsible for Mellette's death had been caught, I felt free to joke again, without the investigation hanging over my head.

At some point, Ambrose ordered another bottle of wine, which featured the same label and also tasted like cherries and licorice. By the time we'd finished our meals, I'd remembered one last detail.

I gently tucked my napkin under my plate. "You know, it turns out Herbert Solomon didn't buy Sweetwater, after all."

"Really?" Ambrose gazed at me, his eyelids heavier now. "Why would he lie about it?"

"Good question. I know he wanted to buy it, and he figured it was only a matter of time. But Ashley wouldn't sell it to him, after all."

"But you said the owner needed the money."

"He did. But once the map sold, he realized maybe he and his brother could survive on that."

Ambrose's eyes widened slightly. "So you're saying it's still on the market?"

"I wish. But, no, it's not." Surprisingly, I wasn't too disappointed after all. I figured I had everything I needed within arm's reach, mansion or not. "He wouldn't sell it to Herbert Solomon, but he agreed to give it to Hank Dupre."

"I didn't know Beatrice's uncle was in the market for a new house."

"He wasn't. That's the best part." I rested my hand on the table, only inches away from Ambrose's. "He only wanted the mansion so he could preserve it. And finally put it on the National Register of Historic Places, where it belonged."

Ambrose's fingers felt warm when he cupped his hand over mine. "I'm sorry. I know you really wanted that place. We would've had a lot of fun renovating it."

"It's okay. I have a feeling we'll find something else to do with our time."

Please turn the page for an exciting sneak peek of
Sandra Bretting's next
Missy DuBois mystery
SOMEONE'S MAD AT THE HATTER
coming soon wherever e-books are sold!

Chapter 1

Maybe it was the sight of so many eyes swimming around in the stockpot that bothered me. I couldn't exactly scoop up the black-eyed peas when they squinted like that. Not to mention the sauce was full of garlic, jalapenos, and onions, which made my nose itch. Whatever the reason, I walked past the pot of good luck peas on the mansion's buffet table and headed for a stack of sweet-milk biscuits instead.

"Missy! Over here." Ambrose waved to me from the other side of the dining room.

I grabbed a biscuit and crossed the room, which was easy, since Mr. Dupre's New Year's Day breakfast had thinned and only a few folks remained.

"Where've you been?" he asked. "And aren't you gonna try the peas?"

"Not this early in the morning." Unlike me, my best-friend-turned-beau had a cast-iron stomach. "I've been here awhile, but I ran across Beatrice and we wanted to catch up."

My assistant, Beatrice, and I had been invited, along with half of Bleu Bayou, to usher in another January at the old Sweetwater mansion, Southern style. Along with black-eyed peas, the buffet held breakfast tacos with collard greens, which folks swore would fatten your wallet, and omelets filled with roast pork, which was another tradition Southerners held near and dear. Not sure how that one started, since it involved pigs and the way they rooted forward in the mud, but, as my granddaddy used to say, "Traditions are what put the sugar in sweet tea."

So come January first, everyone loaded a Chinette plate with cooked greens, roast pork, and swimming peas and hoped for the best.

Ambrose shook his head. "You're missing out."

"It's early. I want to give my stomach a chance to wake up first."

He flashed a crooked smile, which made my heart flip-flop. We'd only recently begun to date, after wasting a perfectly good year and a half as friends and roommates, but my heart couldn't help the palpitations.

His lopsided grin quickly faded, though. "Say, something happened a little while ago. I took a phone call from one of my clients, and she's panicked. Gained fifteen pounds over the holidays and now she's afraid her wedding gown won't fit. I promised I'd meet her at the studio for another fitting."

"Today? But it's New Year's Day!" I popped the biscuit in my mouth. After spending so much time designing wedding gowns for persnickety brides, Ambrose deserved a holiday. Not to mention I'd created enough hats, veils, and fancy headbands to crown every bride from here to the Louisiana border. I quickly chewed and swallowed. "Can't it wait? We never take time off. I was hoping we'd spend the day together."

"Sorry, but it can't. She's paying me fifteen thousand for the gown."

He pecked me on the cheek, and the palpitations began again. *That man always does know how to shut me up.* "Okay. Do what you gotta do."

"I'll be home soon." He held up his hand. "Promise. I'll give her one quick fitting and then I'll head back to the rent house."

Ambrose and I shared what the locals called a "rent house." Although we each had our own bedroom, I hoped one day we might share a *whole* lot more.

"Sounds like you've already made up your mind," I said. "Please come home at some point, though. I know how you get when you're with a client."

"I will." He held up his hand again. "I swear. It'll be a couple hours, max. And I've got a great idea. Why don't you go to your hat studio in the meantime? You can pick up your mail and maybe double check the locks."

Well, that doesn't sound so bad. I'd been meaning to stop by Crowning Glory over the holidays, anyway. But somehow I'd never made it out of fuzzy socks, tattered Vanderbilt T-shirts, and faded yoga pants, which wouldn't be the best advertisement for my business.

Today was different, though. Today I wore a Brooks Brother's blazer, a wool pencil skirt, and brand new boots, so maybe I should make the most of it. "Okay, okay. You're probably right."

He passed me his plate. "I know I am. And here. Eat some peas while I'm gone. I want you to have good luck too."

I accepted the leftovers halfheartedly as he walked away. The fact that we stood in this beautiful dining room at all struck me as lucky enough. Only a few months ago, a greedy property developer tried to snatch the mansion from its heirs and convert it to high-end condos, until a local realtor rode to the rescue. If not for him, we might've been standing in a sales office instead of a formal dining room built in the 1800s.

Speaking of which . . . where was he? Usually there was no mistaking Mr. Dupre, with his colorful dress shirts in their crazy colors.

I quickly scanned the room. Someone in a riot of purple and gold stood across the way, near the kitchen, with his back to me.

I padded over to him. "Good morning, Mr. Dupre." The colors swirled as he whipped around.

"Hello, there! And please call me Hank. Mr. Dupre's my dad. Happy New Year!" Instead of shaking the hand I offered, he grabbed me in a bear hug.

"You too." My voice squeaked. When I recovered, I noticed someone else was standing nearby. The old woman wore a flour thumbprint in the cleft of her chin. "Did you cook for us today, Miss Ruby?"

"*Oui.* Da cornbread and collard greens." She spied the nearly full plate in my hand before I could do anything about it. "And ya barely touched yers. Gah-lee. Ya be gettin' so skinny, betcha don' even throw da shadow." She leaned in close. "I gotta magick potion put soma dat weight back on ya."

"I'm sure you do." Everyone in Bleu Bayou knew about Ruby Oubre and her magick potions. She cooked them up in a singlewide she kept on the banks of the Atchafalaya River. Her specialties included love potions, court case spells, and "gris-gris," which was a traditional voodoo charm.

"Ma oil will put da fat back on ya." She clucked her tongue. "Make yer shadow come round."

"I'm sure it would. But something came up and I should get going. Thanks again for inviting me, uh, Hank."

"You're very welcome." His eyes narrowed. "And be careful out there. Last night's storm left the roads real slick. Don't drive too fast."

"I won't. See you both soon."

As I ducked into the kitchen, I spied a silver garbage bin by the back wall. Good luck was one thing, but eating stone-cold peas was quite another, so I carefully tipped Ambrose's plate into the trash before dashing out the back door.

A cool wind feathered my face the minute I stepped outside. Once I drew the flaps of my blazer closed, I joined a gravel path that led from the back of the mansion to its front, pebbles crunching beneath my feet. Normally, a majestic pin oak blocked the property from the street, but the cold had stripped the tree bare, exposing a line of cars parked grille to fender on the road's shoulder.

Most of them I recognized. One, a battered pickup painted surprisingly pink, was pushed into the gleaming bumper of a Rolls Royce Silver Shadow parked in front of it. Since the pickup belonged to Beatrice, my assistant, I should've been mortified, but the cold urged me to forget about anything but finding my car.

I'd parked my VW all the way on the end, so I rushed to it and fumbled with the door handle until it swung open. Thankfully, the engine started right away, and I drove from the mansion under a blanket of wet, gray skies.

Soon a blurry stretch of sugar cane fields materialized in the windshield, the ground littered with leftover stalks from the fall harvest. While fields and petroleum plants dominated this part of the Mississippi River, most folks pictured antebellum mansions when they heard about the Great River Road. It was understandable, since the farmland and factories couldn't possibly compete with the beautifully restored wedding-cake mansions sandwiched in between them.

A few minutes later, I passed the kitschy neon sign for Dippin' Donuts, where a lighted arrow shot from the roof and pierced the sky. As I passed, I began to mentally compose a to-do list of all the things I wanted to accomplish once I reached my hat studio.

First, I'd scoop up the mail that puddled behind the front door. Next, I'd answer a river of e-mails that no doubt flowed into my computer. I owed several people phone calls, including my accountant, my largest supplier, and the building's landlord. Since that last person had promised to fix a water stain on my studio's ceiling, I mentally moved him to the top of the list.

And while I didn't have any appointments booked for today, I could always leave a few reminder calls for girls coming later in the week.

As soon as I arrived at the studio, I swerved the VW convertible, which I'd nicknamed Ringo, since it *was* a Beetle, after all, into the main parking lot. The landlord provided a separate lot for us employees behind the shops, but the blacktop on that one spit dirt and tar everywhere, which wouldn't be good for Ringo's undercarriage.

I'd discovered this building by accident. It was two stories tall and made of thick, weathered brick on the outside, with the original hardwood plank floors inside. Everyone called it the Factory because the building had once housed a hot-sauce plant. That was before the tabasco companies all hightailed it out of here, except for the most famous one, which still operates out on Avery Island.

Somewhere along the line, an architect added a soaring glass pyramid between my studio's wing and the one across from it to give the building a modern twist. Sort of like the glass prism at the Louvre, rising smackdab from the middle of buildings made centuries before it.

I pulled into the parking lot, which was mostly empty, and parked next to Ambrose's Audi. Once outside the car, I began to make my way to my studio. Normally it was a straight shot, but today I hopscotched over puddles slick with leftover motor oil. Apparently the storm had even ripped a downspout from the wall, and it blocked my path like something tossed there by the Tin Man.

Curious now, I paused. If last night's storm had pulled a metal downspout clear off a brick wall, I had to wonder how much damage it had caused to my roof. A water mark had appeared overnight on a standalone section of ceiling that jutted out from the building. The stain seemed to grow until it reached the size of a Thanksgiving turkey platter.

A call to my landlord definitely was in order. Although . . . he might be more willing to fix it if I could report the actual amount of rainfall. Maybe I'd even embellish the total a bit, although that didn't seem like a very Christian thing to do. Either way, I had a perfect tool to help me build my case.

A few months back, I'd stumbled across a page on Pinterest, the motherlode for do-it-yourself projects, which explained how to make a homemade rain gauge from an old wood base, an ordinary dowel and a glass vial from the hardware store. Since "I cain't-never-could," as we say here in the South, resist the urge to fluff things up a bit, I faux-painted an old hat stand for the base and substituted a ribbon curler's handle for a plain dowel. Then I painted fat raindrops on a clear tube from Homestyle Hardware and *violà!* I'd made a custom rain gauge with an artful twist.

I'd set the creation on a curb in the employee parking lot, right behind my studio. Just in case, I'd also rescued an old whiskey barrel from the trash heap and rolled it nearby for a second opinion. One look at those two, and I'd know how much rainwater to report.

So I rounded the building and came across the empty parking lot, which wasn't surprising, since everyone had probably stayed home with their good-luck peas and cornbread. I hugged the back wall and sidestepped more puddles until I reached the curb behind my studio.

Something was wrong, though. My beautiful rain gauge was gone, and the barrel that normally sat next to it lay on its side. Who'd steal a rain gauge? And, more importantly, how could a few inches of water upend a heavy whiskey barrel like that? I stopped in front of the barrel, where I bent to take a glimpse inside.

A lock of hair flowed from the cask onto the asphalt, like a trail of salt poured over pepper. Not only that, but blood matted the strands.

The scream I let loose no doubt sounded four states away.

Sandra Bretting is a journalist who has written for the *Los Angeles Times*, Houston Chronicle and others. A graduate of the University of Missouri School of Journalism, she turned to writing fiction after twenty years in that field. Her first mystery debuted in 2012. Readers can visit her at www.SandraBretting.com.

MURDER AT MORNINGSIDE

A Missy DuBois Mystery

First in a
New Series!

SANDRA BRETTING

www.ingramcontent.com/pod-product-compliance
Lightning Source LLC
Chambersburg PA
CBHW022152260626
47155CB00017B/1846